Even Conan's lightning quickness failed to avoid the monstrous white form that suddenly hurtled upon him from above. He had a glimpse of shapeless limbs and a horribly featureless head. Then he was flung to the ground with such violence that the breath was knocked out of his lungs.

He struggled madly to free his right hand and slash at his foe with the naked knife in his fist, but even his giant strength seemed like a babe's compared to the demonic power of the monster. And then a horrible, featureless face bent forward, as if to stare straight into his eyes. An abysmal chill began to envelop his body, and he felt a deadly tugging at the borders of his mind. In that amorphous terror he saw mirrored the abysmal evil of the darker gulfs where slavering things dwell, preying on human souls. Forces tore at the roots of his reason; icy drops of sweat sprang out upon his forehead . . .

Chronological order of the CONAN series:

CONAN
CONAN OF CIMMERIA
CONAN THE FREEBOOTER
CONAN THE WANDERER
CONAN THE ADVENTURER
CONAN THE BUCCANEER
CONAN THE WARRIOR
CONAN THE USURPER
CONAN THE CONQUEROR
CONAN THE AVENGER
CONAN OF AQUILONIA
CONAN OF THE ISLES
CONAN THE SWORDSMAN
CONAN THE LIBERATOR
CONAN THE SWORD OF SKELOS
CONAN THE ROAD OF KINGS
CONAN THE REBEL

Illustrated CONAN novels:

CONAN AND THE SORCERER
CONAN: THE FLAME KNIFE
CONAN THE MERCENARY
THE TREASURE OF TRANICOS

Other CONAN novels:

THE BLADE OF CONAN
THE SPELL OF CONAN

CONAN

10

THE AVENGER

BY ROBERT E. HOWARD, BJORN NYBERG,
AND L. SPRAGUE DE CAMP

ACE BOOKS, NEW YORK

Chapters 2 to 5 inclusive of *The Return of Conan* by Björn Nyberg and L. Sprague de Camp were first published as a novella, *Conan the Victorious*, in *Fantastic Universe Science Fiction*, for September, 1957; copyright © 1957 by King-Size Publications, Inc. The entire novel was then published as *The Return of Conan*, N.Y.: Gnome Press, Inc.; copyright © 1957 by Gnome Press.

The Hyborian Age, Part 2, by Robert E. Howard, was originally published in the booklet, *The Hyborian Age*, by the Los Angeles-New York Cooperative Publications, 1938; and in *Skull-Face and Others*, by Robert E. Howard, Sauk City, Wis.: Arkham House, 1946.

CONAN THE AVENGER

An Ace Book / published by arrangement with
Conan Properties, Inc.

PRINTING HISTORY
Original Ace edition / 1968

ISBN: 0-441-11483-0

Ace Books are published by The Berkley Publishing Group,
200 Madison Avenue, New York, New York 10016.
The name "Ace" and the "A" logo
are trademarks belonging to
Charter Communications, Inc.

PRINTED IN THE UNITED STATES OF AMERICA

20   19   18   17   16

3/94

Contents

Pages 8 and 9: A map of the world of Conan in the
Hyborian Age, based upon notes and sketches by Robert
E. Howard and upon previous maps by P. Schuyler Mil-
ler, John D. Clark, David Kyle, and L. Sprague de Camp,
with a map of Europe and adjacent regions superimposed
for reference.

Introduction

CONAN THE CIMMERIAN is the hero of over thirty stories by Robert E. Howard (1906–36 of Cross Plains, Texas), by my colleagues Björn Nyberg and Lin Carter, and by myself. Nyberg, Carter, and I have completed a number of unfinished Howard manuscripts and have written several pastiches, based upon hints in Howard's notes and letters, to fill the gaps in the saga.

The Conan stories are of a kind called "heroic fantasy" or "sword-and-sorcery fiction." Such a story is a tale of swashbuckling adventure with a strong supernatural element, laid in an imaginary world—perhaps this planet as it is once supposed to have been, or as it will be some day, or some other world or dimension—where magic works and modern science and technology are unknown. Here all men are mighty, all women beautiful, all problems simple, and all life adventurous. The genre was developed by William Morris in the late nineteenth century and by Lord Dunsany and Eric R. Eddison in the early twentieth. Notable recent examples are J. R. R. Tolkien's trilogy, *The Lord of the Rings;* Fletcher Pratt's *The Well of the Unicorn;* and Fritz Leiber's stories of Fafhrd and the Gray Mouser.

During the last decade of his short life (1927–36), Howard turned out a large volume of what was then called "pulp fiction"—sport, detective, western, historical, adventure, weird, and ghost stories, besides his poetry and his many fantasies. At the age of thirty, he ended a promising literary career by suicide.

Howard wrote several series of heroic fantasies, most of them published in *Weird Tales*. Of these, the most popular as well as the longest single series has been the Conan stories.

Howard was a natural storyteller, whose narratives are unsurpassed for vivid, gripping, headlong action. His heroes—King Kull, Conan, Bran Mak Morn, Solomon Kane—are larger than life: men of mighty thews, hot passions, and indomitable will, who dominate the tales through which they stride. Withal, as I have learned from editing his works, Howard had an excellent prose style: precise, straightforward, simple, unobtrusive, and highly readable. He had the rare knack of giving the impression of a highly colorful scene without actually using many adjectives to describe it.

Eighteen Conan stories were published during Howard's lifetime. Eight others, from complete manuscripts to mere fragments, have been found among his papers since 1950. Late in 1951, I discovered a cache of Howard manuscripts in the apartment of the then literary agent for Howard's estate. These included a few unpublished Conan stories, which I edited for publication.

The incomplete, open-ended nature of the Conan saga presented an irresistible temptation to add to it as Howard himself might in time have done had he lived. Besides editing the unpublished Conan stories, I undertook, in the early 1950s, to rewrite the manuscripts of four other unpublished Howard adventure stories to convert them into Conan stories. This did not prove difficult, since the heroes were much like Conan, and I had merely to delete anachronisms and introduce a supernatural element.

Meanwhile a citizen and resident of Sweden, Björn Nyberg, took a further step. Introduced to Conan by his friends Ostlund and Chapman, he had been hooked, as so many others have been, in reading of the deeds of the mighty Cimmerian. Nyberg had the courage to sit down and write a whole novel about Conan, in a language that was not his mother tongue. This endeavor resulted in a collaboration between Nyberg and myself, the outcome of which was "The Return of Conan" herein.

Howard's Conan stories are laid about twelve thousand years ago in the imaginary Hyborian Age, eight thousand years after the sinking of Atlantis and seven thousand years before the beginnings of recorded history. A gigantic barbarian adventurer from the backward northern land of Cimmeria, Conan arrived as a youth in the kingdom of Zamora (see map) and for several years made a precarious living there and in neighboring lands as a thief. After a gore-spattered career as mercenary soldier, pirate, treasure hunter, and chief of various barbarian tribes, he became a scout on the western frontier of Aquilonia, fighting the savage Picts. After rising to command in the Aquilonian army and defeating a Pictish invasion, Conan was lured back to Tarantia, the capital, and imprisoned by the jealous King Numedides. Escaping, he was chosen to lead a revolution against the degenerate king. Conan slew Numedides and took the throne for his own, to become ruler of the mightiest Hyborian Kingdom.

Conan soon found that being king was no bed of houris. A cabal of discontented nobles almost succeeded in assassinating him. By a ruse, the kings of Koth and Ophir trapped and imprisoned him, but he escaped in time to turn the tables on these would-be conquerors of Aquilonia.

Other enemies conjured an ancient wizard back from the grave and, with the help of this living-dead sorcerer, broke Aquilonia's armies and drove Conan into exile. But again he returned to confound and destroy his foes.

In the process, Conan acquired a queen, with whom he settled down happily, dismissing his harem of concubines. For about a year, his reign was more or less peaceful. But then another foe gathered his forces to strike . . .

And here the present story begins. At this time, Conan was about forty-six or forty-seven years old, showing few signs of age save the scars that crisscrossed his mighty frame and a more cautious, deliberate approach to adventure and revelry than had been the case in his riotous youth.

When Howard began writing the Conan stories in 1932, he gave serious thought to the setting—his "Hyborian Age" civilization. To fix it firmly in his own mind, he wrote an essay in which he set forth the pseudo-history of prehistoric times that he used as a background for the stories. In the last year of his life, he submitted this essay for publication in a fan magazine, *The Phantagraph*, with an apologetic note explaining that this was purely a fictional device to enable him to make the Conan stories internally consistent. It was not to be taken seriously as setting forth his true beliefs about the prehistory of mankind.

The first half of *The Hyborian Age* was published in *The Phantagraph* before that periodical ceased publication. The whole essay was then published in 1938 in a mimeographed booklet, *The Hyborian Age*, put out by a group of science-fiction fans. The first half, which carries this pseudo-history down to the time of Conan, was reprinted in *Conan*, chronologically the first volume of the present series. The second half, which begins after Conan's time and continues down to the beginnings of recorded history, is reproduced here.

L. Sprague de Camp

THE RETURN OF CONAN

by
Björn Nyberg and L. Sprague de Camp

For two months after the battle of Tanasul, which destroyed the Nemedian conquerors of Aquilonia and their sorcerous ally Xaltotun, Conan is kept furiously busy by the tasks of reorganizing his kingdom, repairing the damage done by the invaders, and collecting the promised indemnity from Nemedia.

Then Conan prepares to visit Nemedia, to return the captured King Tarascus to his homeland and to fetch back to Aquilonia the girl Zenobia, who saved his life when he was imprisoned in the dungeons of the palace at the Nemedian capital of Belverus. Before his departure, he tactfully dismisses his harem of shapely concubines. With his usual chivalry towards women, he makes a point of finding them husbands— or at least other protectors—before bidding them farewell.

The journey to and from Belverus is a triumphal procession without untoward incident. Back in Tarantia, Conan celebrates his wedding to Zenobia with all the pomp of which a rich and ancient kingdom is capable. Between the pressure of state business and his absorption in Zenobia, the next few months pass swiftly for Conan. Those who know him best are a

*little surprised to see the king, in middle age, turn
monogamous and even uxorious; but the moody, met-
tlesome Cimmerian has always been unpredictable.
Then, however . . .*

—*"Know furthermore, O Prince, that Conan the
barbarian thus won at last to great fame and high
estate as king of Aquilonia, the starry gem of the
green West with its gallant nobles, sturdy warriors,
intrepid frontiersmen, and beauteous damsels. But
dark and terrible forces were at work to rock his
throne and wreck his fortune. For, on the night of the
feast at Tarantia to celebrate the year of peace
that followed the overthrow of the conspiracy of
Valerius, Tarascus, and Amalric, and the destruction of the wizard Xaltotun, Conan's lately-wedded
queen Zenobia was snatched from the palace by a
winged shape out of nightmare and borne off eastward. Thinking it better to travel swiftly, namelessly,
and alone than to take an army with him, Conan
set out in search of his stolen mate . . ."*

THE NEMEDIAN CHRONICLES.

16

Prologue

THE CHAMBER was murky. Long, flaming tapers, set in iron brackets in the walls of stone, dispelled the gloom but little. It was difficult to discern the robed and hooded figure at the unadorned table in the middle of the floor. It was even harder to see the outlines of another form, huddled in the darkness, seemingly engaged in muted speech with the first one.

There was a gust of wind through the room, like the sweep of giant wings. The tapers flickered madly, and the figure at the table was suddenly alone.

1. Wings of Darkness

THE FORBIDDING WALLS of the royal palace at Tarantia rose in jagged silhouette against the darkening sky. Watchmen strode along the battlements, halberd on shoulder and sword on hip, but their vigilance was relaxed. Their eyes strayed often toward the entrance of the palace. Over the lowered drawbridge and under the raised portcullis, gay-clad knights and nobles entered with their ladies.

The sharp eye could discern Prospero, the king's general and right-hand man, arrayed in crimson velvet with golden Poitainian leopards worked upon his jupon. His long legs measured his strides in high boots of the finest Kordavan leather. There went Pallantides, commander of the Black Dragons, in light armor later to be doffed; Trocero, hereditary count of Poitain, his slim waist and erect carriage belying the silver in his hair; the counts of Manara and Couthen, the barons of Lor and Imirus and many more. All went in with fair ladies in rich silks and satins, while their retainers removed the litters and gilded chariots in which their masters had been conveyed.

Peace reigned in Aquilonia. It had prevailed for more than a year since the last attempt of the king of Nemedia, aided by the revived Acheronian wizard Xaltotun, to wrest the kingdom from Conan. Years before, in his turn, Conan had torn the crown from the bloody head of the tyrant Numedides, whom he slew on the very throne.

But the Nemedian scheme had failed. Heavy damages were exacted, and the withered mummy of the dead Xaltotun was borne away on his mysterious chariot to haunts dark and unknown. King Conan's power waxed stronger and stronger, the more his people became aware of the wisdom and justice of his rule. The only disorders were the intermittent raids of the savage Picts on the western border. These, however, were held in check by seasoned troops on the Thunder River.

This was a night of feasting. Torches flared in rows about the gate; colorful carpets from Turan covered the coarse flagstones. Gaily-clad servants flitted about, guided and spurred by shouts from the major-domos. This was the night when King Conan gave a royal ball in honor of his queen, Zenobia, one-time slave girl in the Nemedian king's seraglio. She had aided Conan to escape when he lay a prisoner in the dungeons of Belverus and had been rewarded by the highest honor that could be conferred on a woman of the western lands. She became queen of Aquilonia, the mightiest kingdom west of Turan.

Wen could the glittering throng of guests observe the ardent love that bound the royal sovereigns to each other. It was apparent in gestures, mannerisms, and speech, though Conan's barbarian blood probably urged him to do away with civilized dissimulation and crush his lovely queen in his strong arms. Instead, he stood at arm's length from her, answering bows and curtseys with an ease which seemed natural but was really newly acquired.

Ever and anon, though, the king's eyes strayed toward the far wall, where hung an array of splendid weapons—swords, spears, axes, maces, and javelins. Much as the king loved to see his people at peace, no less could he curb the urge of his barbarian heritage to see red blood flow and to feel the crunch of an enemy's armor and bones beneath the edge of his heavy broadsword. But now it was time for peaceful pursuits. Conan let his eyes wander back to linger briefly on the fair countess curtseying before him.

Fair were the ladies, and a judge would be sorely put to decide a contest for beauty—at least, if he were choosing among the guests. For, in truth, the queen was more beautiful than anyone. The perfection of her form was outlined by the clinging, low-necked gown she wore, with only a silver circlet to confine the foamy mass of her wavy black hair. Moreover, her perfectly-molded face radiated such innate nobility and kindliness as were seldom seen in those times.

However, if the king was counted fortunate by his fellow men, no less was Queen Zenobia envied by the ladies. Conan cut an imposing figure in his simple black tunic, with legs clothed in black hose and feet booted in soft, black leather. The golden lion of Aquilonia blazed upon his breast. Otherwise his sole ornament was the slender golden circlet on his square-cut black mane. Looking at the great spread of his massive shoulders, his lean waist and hips, and his legs muscled with a tiger's deadly power, one could see that this was no man born to civilization.

But Conan's most arresting features were the smoldering blue eyes in his dark, scarred face, inscrutable, with depths no one could plumb. Those same eyes had seen things undreamed of by this gay throng, had looked on battlefields strewn with mangled corpses, decks running red with blood, barbarous executions, and secret rites at the altars of monstrous

20

deities. His powerful hands had swung the western broadsword, the Zuagir tulwar, the Zhaibar knife, the Turanian yataghan, and the forester's ax with the same devastating skill and power against men of all races and against inhuman beings from dark and nameless realms. The veneer of civilization lay thin over his barbaric soul.

The ball began. King Conan opened it with his queen in the first complicated steps of the Aquilonian minuet. Though he was no expert at the more intricate figures of the dance, the primordial instincts of the barbarian took to the rhythm of the melody with an ease and smoothness that enhanced the results of hurried lessons given during the past week by the court's sweating master of ceremonies. Everyone in the glittering throng followed suit. Soon couples milled colorfully on the mosaic floor.

Thick candles cast a warm, soft light over the hall. Nobody noticed the silent draft that began to waft through the air, causing the flames of one chandelier to tremble and flicker. Nobody noticed, either, the burning eyes that peered from a window niche, sweeping an avid glance over the crowd. Their glare fastened upon the slim, silver-sheathed figure in the king's arms. Only the burning eyes were to be seen, but a soft, gloating chuckle whispered through the darkness. Then the eyes disappeared and the casement closed.

The great bronze gong at the end of the hall boomed, announcing a pause. The guests, hot from dancing, sat down to refresh themselves with iced wine and Turanian sherbet.

"Conan! I want a nip of fresh air; all this dancing has made me hot." The queen flung the words over her shoulder as she made her way toward the now open doors to the broad balcony.

The king started to follow but was detained by a score of ladies begging him to tell them of his early life. Was it true that he had been a chieftain of wild hordes in half-fabulous Ghulistan in the Himelian Mountains? Was it he who by a daring stroke had saved the kingdom of Khauran from the Shemite plunderers of the mercenary captain Constantius? Had he once been a pirate?

Questions like these flew like hailstones. Conan answered them curtly or evasively. His barbarian instincts made him restive. They had prompted him to accompany Zenobia out upon the balcony to guard her, even though no danger could threaten his beloved spouse here, in his capital, in his own castle, surrounded by friends and loyal soldiers.

Still he felt uneasy. There was a feeling in his blood of impending danger and doom. Trusting his animal instincts, he began to make his way toward the doors of the balcony despite the beseeching wails of his lovely audience.

Elbowing his way forward a bit more brusquely than became a king, Conan caught sight of the silver figure of Zenobia. Her back was toward him, her hair moving in the soft, cool breeze. He grunted with relief. For once, it seemed, his senses had deluded him. Nonetheless he continued forward.

Suddenly, the slim form of the queen was shrouded in night. A black pall fell over the company. Secret words were mumbled into handkerchiefs by painted lips and bearded mouths. An icy breath of doom swept through the hall. The ground trembled with thunder. The queen screamed.

When the darkness fell, Conan sprang like a panther for the balcony doors, upsetting noble guests and wine-laden tables. Another cry was heard. The sound dwindled, as if Zenobia were being carried

22

away. The king reached the balcony to find it empty.

Conan's glance sought the unscalable sides of the palace and saw nothing. Then he lifted his gaze. There, limned against the moonlit sky, he saw a fantastic shape, a horrible anthropomorphic nightmare, clasping the silvery glint that was his beloved wife. Carried along by powerful beats of its batlike wings, the monster shrank to a dot on the eastern horizon.

Conan stood for a moment, a statue of black steel. Only his eyes seemed alive with icy rage and terrible despair. When he turned his gaze to the audience, they shrank back as if he had become the very monster that had carried off his queen. Without a word, he went out of the hall, scattering people, tables, and chairs heedlessly before him.

At the exit he paused before the weapon-laden wall and tore down a plain but heavy broadsword, which had served him well in many campaigns. As he lifted the blade, he spoke words thick with emotion:

"From this hour, I am no longer your king until I have returned with my stolen queen. If I cannot defend my own mate, I am not fit to rule. But, by Crom, I will seek out this robber and wreak vengeance upon him, be he protected by all the armed hosts in the world!"

Then the king opened his mouth to voice a weird and terrible call that echoed shudderingly through the hall. It rang like the cry of doomed souls. The eerie horror of its tones made many a face turn ashen.

The king was gone.

Prospero hurried after Conan. Trocero paused, surveying all, before he, too, followed.

A trembling Poitainian countess voiced the question that pressed the minds of many guests. "What was that terrible shout? It froze the blood in my veins. I felt as if a frightful doom were upon me. The avenging souls of the Dark Lands must scream like that when they roam the barren wastes for their prey."

The gray-haired count of Raman, veteran of border wars, answered: "Your guess is close enough, milady. It is the battle cry of the Cimmerian tribes. It is voiced only when they are about to fling themselves into battle with utter abandon and no concern other than to kill." He paused. "I have heard it once before—at the bloody sack of Venarium, when the black-haired barbarians swarmed over the walls despite our arrow storm and put everybody to the sword."

Silence fell over the throng.

"No, Prospero, no!" Conan's heavy fist thundered down upon the table. "I will travel alone. To draw armored legions from the realm might tempt attack by some scheming foe. Tarascus has not forgotten the beating we gave him, and Koth and Ophir are untrustworthy as always. I shall ride, not as King Conan of Aquilonia, with a shining retinue of lords and lancers, but as Conan of Commeria, the common adventurer."

"But Conan," said Prospero with the easy familiarity that obtained between him and the king, "we cannot let you risk your life on such an uncertain quest. In this manner you may never attain your goal, whereas with the lances of Poitainian knights at your back you can brave any foe. Let us ride with you!"

Conan's blue eyes glowed with fierce appreciation, but he shook his black-maned head. "No, my friend. I feel I am destined to free my queen alone. Even the help of my trusty knights will not assure success. You shall command the army in my absence, and Trocero shall rule the kingdom. If I am not back in two years —choose a new king!"

Conan lifted the slender golden circlet from his black hair and put it on the oaken table. He stood for a moment, brooding.

Trocero and Prospero made no attempt to break the silence. They had long ago learned that Conan's ways were sometimes queer and unfathomable to civilized men. With his barbarian mind unsullied by civilized life, he was apt to let his thoughts run along paths other than the common ones. Here stood not only a king whose queen had been abducted. Here stood the primordial man, whose mate had been torn from him by forces dark and unknown, and who, without show or bluster, was silently storing terrible vengeance in his heart.

With a shrug of his broad shoulders, Conan broke the silence. "A horse, Prospero, and the harness of a common mercenary! I ride at once."

"Whither?" asked the general.

"To the sorcerer Pelias of Koth, who dwells in Khanyria, in Khoraja. I smell black sorcery in to-night's happenings. That flying creature was no earthly bird. I care not for wizards and would rather manage without their help, but now I need Pelias' advice."

Outside the heavy oaken door, a man stood with his ear pressed to the panel. At these words, a smile spread over his features. With a furtive glance, he melted into one of the niches, overhung with heavy draperies, that lined the corridor. He heard the door open. Conan and his friends passed, their footfalls dwindling down the staircase.

The spy waited till the sounds had died. Then, looking right and left, he slunk out of hiding. Garbed in the dress of a retainer of the court, he crossed the courtyard without being challenged. He disappeared into the servants' quarters and soon emerged, donning a heavy woollen cloak against the chill of night. He gave the password to the guard and was let out. He set out for the western part of the city.

Nobody followed him. The smaller streets and lanes were black as the inside of a chimney. Few rays of the clouded moon pierced their murk. Watchmen, bill on shoulder and peaked helmet on head, paced the streets in pairs, talking in low voices. Harlots leaned out of their windows and called to the wanderer. Some were beautiful, showing off the splendor of their white necks by low-cut gowns or sheer silken wraps. Others had haggard and sleazy faces coated with powder and Hyrkanian rouge. But the man hurried on without swerving from his path.

At last he came to a large house in a parklike garden. A high wall surrounded it on all sides, but into a niche was recessed a small door. He knocked four times. The door was opened by a giant, dusky Stygian clad in white. The two men whispered a few words. Then the palace servant hastened toward the house, where all windows were dark but one.

Evidently this was not the house of a native Aquilonian. Heavy tapestries and rich paintings adorned the walls, but the motifs depicted were western. Domed marble temples, white zikkurats, and people with turbaned heads and flowing robes dominated the rich pageantry of gold and silver thread, of silk and satin and curved swords. Arabesqued oval tables, divans with spreads of red and green silks, golden vases with exotic flowers combined to lend an air of the opulent and exotic East.

Resting on a divan, a big, florid man sipped wine

from a jeweled goblet. He returned the salaam of the palace servant with a careless nod.

"What brings you, Marinus?" There was asperity in the languid voice. "Have you not enough work to do for me at the king's ball? It does not end until early morning, unless Conan has called it off in one of his barbaric moods. What has happened?" Taking another sip, he regarded Marinus with a piercing stare.

"Ghandar Chen, my lord, the queen of Aquilonia has been abducted by an unearthly monster, which flew away with her into the sky! The king rides alone tonight to search for her. First, however, to get some clue to the whereabouts of the reaver, he will visit the Kothian sorcerer Pelias in Khanyria."

"By Erlik, this is news indeed!" Ghandar Chen sprang up, eyes blazing. "Five of my poisoners hang on the hill of execution, so much kite's meat. Those damned martinets of the Black Dragons are incorruptible. But now Conan will be alone, in foreign lands!"

He clapped his hands. The Stygian entered silently and stood at attention, his dark visage somber and inscrutable. Ghandar Chen spoke:

"Conan of Aquilonia embarks tonight on a long journey. He rides alone, as a common mercenary. His first goal will be the city of Khanyria in Khoraja, where he will seek the assistance of the sorcerer Pelias. Ride swiftly to Baraccus, who camps on the Yivga River. Order him to take as many trustworthy men as he needs and slay Conan in Khanyria. The Cimmerian must not reach Pelias. If that cursed necromancer chooses to help him, he might blast all our men from the earth with a wave of his hand!"

The Stygian's somber eyes flashed, and his usually immobile features were split by a dreadful smile.

"Well do I know Conan," he rumbled, "since he crushed the host of Prince Kutamun outside Khoraja. I was one of the few survivors, later to be captured by Kothic slavers and sold—I, born a noble and bred to war and the hunt! Long have I waited for my revenge! If the gods permit, I will slay the Cimmerian myself." His hand sought the hilt of his long dagger. "I go at once, master." He salaamed deeply and left.

Ghandar Chen seated himself at a richly-inlaid rosewood table. From the drawer he took a golden pen and parchment. He wrote:

To King Yezdigerd, lord of Turan and the Eastern Empire. From your faithful servant Ghandar Chen, greetings. Conan the Cimmerian, the *kozak* and pirate, rides alone for Khanyria. I have sent word to slay him there. When it is done, I will send you his head. Should he by some magical feat escape, his road will probably run through Turanian territory. Written in the Year of the Horse, on the third day of the Golden Month.

He signed and sanded it. The Turanian then rose and gave the parchment to Marinus, who had been lolling in the background. He snapped:

"Ride swiftly eastward. Start at once. My servants will furnish you with arms and a horse. You shall take this to King Yezdigerd himself in Aghrapur. He will reward us both handsomely."

A satisfied smile was upon Ghandar Chen's face as he sank back upon the divan, his hand reaching for the goblet again.

2. The Ring of Rakhamon

THE SCORCHING AFTERNOON SUN cast searing rays
across the desert like whiplashes of white fire. Distant
groves of palm trees shimmered; flocks of vultures
hung like clumps of ripe, black grapes in the foliage.
Endless expanses of yellow sand stretched as far as
the eye could see in undulating dunes and flats of
ultimate aridity.

A solitary rider halted his horse in the shade of the
palm fronds that fringed an oasis. Though he wore
the snowy *khalat* of the desert-dwellers, his features
belied any thought of Eastern origin. The hand that
shaded his questing eyes was broad and powerful
and ridged with scars. His skin was browned, not
with the native duskiness of the Zuagir, but with the
ruddy bronze of the sunbaked Westerner. The eyes
were a volcanic blue, like twin pools of unplumbable
depth. A glint at his sleeve betrayed the fact that the
traveler wore a coat of mail under his flowing dress.
At his side hung a long, straight sword in a plain
leather scabbard.

Conan had ridden far and fast. Plunging across
country with reckless speed, he had broken four horses
on his way to Koth. Having reached the expanses of
desert that formed the eastern end of the Kothian
kingdom, he had paused to buy a khalat and some
bread and meat at a dingy, dirty-white border village. Nobody had barred his way, though many an

unkempt head was thrust through a door in wonder at the speed of this lonely rider, and many an armored guardsman stroked his beard, pondering on this mercenary's haste.

There were, indeed, few in the Kothic realm who would have recognized King Conan of Aquilonia, for between the mutually hostile Aquilonians and Kothians there was little intercourse.

Conan's sharp eyes swept the horizon. In the shimmering distance he detected the faint outlines of domed buildings and towering walls. This, then, would be the town of Khanyria in the kingdom of Khoraja. Here he would seek the help of Pelias the sorcerer in recovering his stolen queen. Five years before, he had met and befriended Pelias when the Kothian wizard lay imprisoned in the vaults of the scarlet citadel of his foe Tsotha-lanti.

Conan spurred the black stallion toward the distant towers. "Crom!" he muttered. "I hope Pelias is in his full senses. Like as not he's lying drunk on his golden divan, dead to the world. But, by Badb, I'll waken him!"

In the narrow streets and cobbled marketplace of Khanyria, a motley throng swirled and eddied. Zuagirs from the desert villages to the northeast, swaggering mercenaries with roving eyes and hands on hilts, hawkers crying their wares, harlots in red kirtles and painted faces milled together in a flamboyant tableau. Now and then the crowd was riven by the armored retainers of a wealthy noble, his perfumed sedan chair bobbing on the shoulders of ebon-skinned, ox-muscled Kushite slaves. Or a troop of guardsmen clattered out from the barracks, accoutrements clanking and horsehair plumes flowing.

Crassides, the burly captain of the guard at the

Western Gate, stroked his graying beard and muttered. Strangers often passed into the city, but seldom such curious strangers as today's arrivals. Early this afternoon, in a cloud of dust stirred up from the desert sands, had come a troop of seven. The rider in the lead was a lean fellow of vulture look, his narrow mustache framing a thin line of mouth. He was armed like a Western knight, though his cuirass and helm were plain, without any device. By his side rode a huge Stygian on a black horse. A khalat enshrouded the Stygian's form, and his only visible weapon was a massive war bow.

The other five were all well armored, wearing serviceable swords and daggers at their sides and holding lances in their hands. They looked like hardy rogues, as ready to slit a throat as to bounce a wench.

It was not the custom of the Khanyrian city guard to stop strangers without good reason, for here East and West met to mingle, haggle, and trade tall tales. Nevertheless, Crassides cast a searching glance at the seven as they jingled away towards the northern quarter. They disappeared into the profusion of smoky taverns with mongrels yapping about their horses' hooves.

The rest of the day passed quietly, but now it seemed that the trickle of odd strangers must go on. As the sun flung its last rays across the darkening heavens, a tall, burnoosed foreigner reined in before the closed gate and demanded entrance.

Crassides, called to the gate by one of the guards on duty, arrived just as the remaining guard shouted down: "What seek you here, rogue? We let no outlanders in at night to cut our throats and debauch our women! State your name and errand before I clap you in irons!"

31

The stranger's glowing eyes, half hidden beneath his kaffia, regarded the trooper icily. "My friend," said the stranger in a barbarous accent, "for words less than those I have slit a hundred gullets. Let me in or, by Crom, I'll raise a horde to sack this bunch of hovels!"

"Not so fast!" said Crassides, thrusting the guard aside. "Get down, you young fool, and I'll teach you how to speak to strangers later. Now, you, sir!" He spoke to the horseman. "We want no quarrels in Khanyria, and as you see the gate is closed for the night. Ere we open it, you must account for yourself."

"Call me Arus," growled the stranger. "I seek Pelias the sorcerer."

"Let him in," said Crassides. The heavy bolts were drawn. Two watchmen strained at the bronze handles, and one of the door valves swung slowly open. The stranger cantered through, not even glancing at those around the gate. He headed for the northern district, and the click of his horse's hoofs dwindled in the distance.

The discomfited young guard spoke to his captain with restrained heat: "Why do we let this insolent lout ride in as if he were lord of the city? Why not put a shaft through his ribs?"

Crassides smiled through his beard. "Years may teach you wisdom, though I doubt it. Have you never heard how, years ago, a northern barbarian like this one was captured by the warlord of one of the little city-states of Shem to the south? And how he escaped, rounded up a band of outlaw Zuagirs, and came back for vengeance? And how the savage horde stormed the city, putting the people to the sword, flaying captives in the public square, and burning everything except the pole on which the warlord's head was stuck? This fellow might be one of that sort.

"But alone, he can do us little harm. And if he mean us ill, Pelias will know it by his arcane arts and take measures. Now do you begin to see?"

Conan knew that Pelias lurked in a tower of yellow stone at the northern end of the city. He planned to visit the wizard first and later to seek board and lodging. Anything would do. His body and tastes had not been softened by his years of civilized life. A loaf of bread, a hunk of meat, and a jack of foaming ale were all he wanted. For sleep, why, he could use the floor of a tavern if all else failed.

Conan had no wish to spend the night in Pelias' abode, for all its luxury. Too many dark and nameless things were apt to stalk the nighted corridors of the sorcerer's dwelling . . .

There came a muffled oath and a cry of fear. A door to the right flew open, and a young girl flung herself into the street.

Conan reined in. The girl was shaped like one of the *mekhrani* that people the pleasure houses in the paradise of Erlik's true believers. This Conan could readily see, for her simple dress was torn to tatters, leaving her but scantily covered. Brushing back the jet-black tangle of hair from her face, she cast a terrified glance towards the door, which had closed behind her. Then her large eyes turned to Conan, sitting his horse like a statue. Her hand flew to her mouth in terror.

"Now, lass, what's eating you?" spoke the Cimmerian roughly, bending forward. "Is your lover cross with you, or what?"

The girl rose with a lithe motion. "Two drunken soldiers tried to rape me. I came to buy wine for my father. They took my money, too!"

Conan's eyes flashed as he jumped to the ground.

His barbaric code of chivalry made him hate a man's inflicting wanton brutality on a woman.

"Steady, lass. We'll pull their beards yet. Just open the door. Are they the only guests?"

Nodding in terrified confirmation, she led him to the tavern. After a moment's hesitation she opened the door. In two long strides Conan was inside. The door clicked shut behind him.

But no such scene as he had expected confronted him. Here were no drunken soldiers to be quieted by a couple of buffets. Seven alert armed men ranged the walls, swords and daggers gleaming in their hands. The determination to kill was in their eyes as they instantly rushed upon Conan.

A civilized man would have been stunned by surprise one second and cut down in the next, but not the giant Cimmerian. His keen primitive instincts gave him a flash of warning as he crossed the threshold, and his lightning reflexes went instantly into action. No time now to draw the great sword; before he had it out, they would be upon him like a pack of wolves. His only chance lay in instant attack, surprising his attackers by its very boldness before they could ring him and close with him.

A mighty kick sent a bench whirling against the legs of three of his adversaries as they rushed forward. They fell in a clattering, cursing tangle. Conan ducked a whistling sword stroke of one of the other four and smashed his right fist into the man's face before the latter could recover his balance. Conan felt the man's bones crack under the blow, which cast him back against his advancing comrades.

Taking advantage of the confusion, the Cimmerian burst clean through the ring of foes, wheeled with the speed of a panther, grabbed a heavy oaken table and, with a muscle-wrenching heave, hurled it into the faces of his enemies. Weapons clattered to the floor, and oaths and cries of pain rent the air. The lull in the fight gave Conan time to rip the great sword from its sheath and snatch out his dagger with his left hand

He did not wait for a renewed attack. His barbarian blood was roused by this treacherous ambush. A red mist swam before his eyes, and his mind was crazed with the lust of killing. Rushing in to attack, single-handed against the six who were still in action, Conan with a furious kick caved in the ribs of one rascal still on hands and knees. As he parried a thrust with his dagger, a savage swipe of his heavy sword sheared off the sword arm of another. Arm and sword fell to the floor, and the man crumpled up, glassy-eyed and screaming, with blood spurting.

That left four, advancing warily in a half-circle. The tall, wolfish leader feinted at Conan's legs but almost lost his head to the Cimmerian's whistling countercut. He escaped by throwing himself to the floor. Just before he did so, Conan recognized the man as Baraccus, an Aquilonian noble he had exiled for plotting with the Ophireans.

At that instant, the other three rushed in. One desperate sword-stroke caught Conan on the helmet, denting it and dizzying him. Stars swam before his eyes, but he ripped viciously upward and was rewarded by a hoarse, gurgling scream. A .dagger point broke on the stout links of mail covering his right side, but a sword gashed his left arm.

When he hastily wiped the blood from his face he saw that he faced but one enemy, as the Stygian, his dagger broken, had stepped back to pick up a weapon from the floor. The tall leader was rising from his fall.

Conan stepped forward to close with his foe, but

his foot slipped in a pool of blood. He fell heavily.

The assassin confronting him shrieked in triumph and rushed forward, lifting his sword. Conan's foot lashed out and knocked the man's leg from under him, so that his blow went awry and he fell on top of the Cimmerian, impaling himself on the dagger that Conan thrust up to meet his falling form.

Conan flung the body aside and, with catlike speed, sprang again to his feet to meet the attack of the rearmed Stygian. The dusky giant rushed towards Conan, eyes blazing with dark fires and lips foaming with impassioned hatred. Ducking the swipe of the Cimmerian's sword, he whipped his white cloak around the blade, imprisoning it in the heavy folds. The knife that the Stygian had picked up was driven against Conan's side with such force that mail links snapped and the point pierced the Cimmerian's body. But Conan ripped into the brown torso with swift and murderous thrusts of his own dirk. The Stygian's mouth flew open in awful pain, his dagger clattered to the floor, and he doubled up and followed it.

Conan tore his sword free from the folds of the Stygian's dress and advanced upon the unwounded leader. "You've forgotten your knightly oaths since I kicked you off your estate, eh, Baraccus?" he snarled. "I should have had your head when I found out your treason, but this time will do as well as any!"

Conan presented a terrible aspect. From beneath his dented helmet, blood flowed down the side of his sweaty face. His right side was red with gore, and a bloody rent showed in his mailshirt. But the will to kill burned unquenched in his terrible glance. Baraccus, remembering the horrific legends of the Cimmerian's former deeds, lost his nerve and whirled to flee. With a grating laugh, Conan tossed up his sword, caught the hilt reversed, and hurled the weapon like a javelin.

36

The point smashed through the backplate of Baraccus' corselet. Baraccus pitched forward at full length, the sword standing upright in his back and a stream of blood running from his mouth.

Conan relaxed a little, surrounded by enemies dead or unconscious. Then a voice behind him aroused his barbarian senses. He wheeled in a flash, expecting another attack.

A fat man stood in the back door, wringing his pudgy hands. "Oh, mercy, what has happened to my fine house?" he wailed, his face creased by worry. "Blood all over! Furniture ruined!"

Two strides brought Conan to the taverner, under whose chin he poised the point of his dagger. "You had a hand in this, you yapping dog!" he roared. "They could not have set this ambush without your help."

"Mercy, lord! They threatened to cut my throat otherwise! That would have been almost better than this! They said it would be swift and silent . . ."

Conan slapped the man's face with such force that the taverner was thrown against the door jamb. He reeled, and blood ran down his chin from a cut lip.

"Silence!" rumbled Conan, his anger appeased a little. "Be glad I don't flay you an inch at a time!"

"Yes-yes, lord!" The man wept, in abject terror.

"Now fetch a jack of wine, before I split your head! And of the best! Also some clean cloths to bind up these scratches."

As the terrified taverner hurried off, Conan kicked a corpse out of the way and sank down wearily upon a bench. A thought struck him. Where was the handsome wench who had started all this? She was not in the room.

The host returned on trembling legs, holding a flask and a pewter goblet. With an impatient curse, Conan tore the bottle from him and upended it over his parched gullet. When the whole of the contents had poured down without interruption, to the wonder of the unwilling host, Conan set down the empty container with a crash, wiped his mouth on his bloody sleeve, and turned his blue eyes upon the man.

"Killing dries a man's throat," he said. "Now tell me: Where is the girl who was here with these men before I entered?"

The fat taverner, green with fear, shook his head. "Noble lord, I never saw her until she came here yesterday, dressed in outlandish garments. She changed her garb in her room on the upper floor. I know not her name or aught else about her."

Conan heaved himself to his feet, only a little troubled by wounds that would have incapacitated an ordinary man for days. Tearing his sword out of Baraccus' body, he thundered: "Lead me to her room at once! And should this prove another trap, your soul will rot on the black floors of Hell within the instant!"

Knees knocking, the flabby Khanyrian led the way up the narrow stair. The Cimmerian followed, his eyes scanning every cranny with wolfish wariness. On the upper floor, his guide paused before a door and chose a key from the great bunch at his girdle. He unlocked the door and opened it wide to reassure the edgy barbarian.

Conan decided that there was no chance of another ambush in that narrow room. The only furniture was a bed and a small table. On the bed lay green silks, a golden sash, a turban strip with an emerald pin, and a filmy veil. Conan stood silent with startled recognition. This was the garb of a Hyrkanian noblewoman, from the great and growing eastern empire of Turan—from Akif, Shahpur, or Aghrapur itself.

Wheeling and retracing his steps, Conan pondered this new enigma with clouded brow.

With nostrils flaring and sword in hand, Conan stepped alertly from the tavern door. His limbs had become a little stiffened from his wounds and his side ached from the dagger thrust, but he still had vigor enough to spring into the saddle of his waiting horse.

He was mystified by the assault. He well knew that many men of different creeds, races, and stations thirsted for his blood and would have loved to roast his guts over a slow fire. On this mission, however, he had ridden swiftly, silently, and anonymously. Only Trocero and Prospero knew which way he was going, and their loyalty was beyond question. Yet armored foes had ambushed him with gleaming blades. Something or someone had brought Baraccus from the West and the Hyrkanian woman from the East together to try to trap him.

Conan shrugged the puzzle from his mind with the fatalistic equanimity of the barbarian. As he could not now grasp the whole picture behind the recent incident, he was content to wait until further information came to light.

He cantered leisurely through the streets with eyes darting into the shadows. The only light came from an occasional flickering taper in a window. His thoughts came back to the beautiful woman who had nearly led him to his death. The sight of her well-molded form had fired his blood, and he had meant to take a kiss at the very least as a reward for helping her. But now she was gone as if by magic.

Emerging upon a wide, deserted square, Conan,

aided by the dim light of the clouded moon, saw the outline of a spired edifice, pointing like a finger to the heavens. In the deepening darkness it gleamed dull yellow like the reflex of a dying sun. This was the tower where Pelias secreted himself from the undesired company of his fellow men.

A broad expanse of trimmed gardens and lawns surrounded the yellow tower. No walls, fences, or forbidding gates ringed it. They were not needed. Horrid legends, whispered in the dark of evening, had taught the Khanyrians to keep away from sorcerers' abodes, into which an intruder might enter but from which he would probably never return.

Conan's horse shied at the edge of the lawn, whinnying and stomping. It chewed its bit and blew foam from its lips.

"Crom!" muttered the Cimmerian. "It seems as if Pelias has unholy company. Well, I can walk."

He dismounted and strode up the narrow flagstone walk, his eyes roving and his hand on his hilt. Necromantic rites often drew nameless monstrosities in the night, as the smell of carrion attracts vultures. Conan had met many kinds of beings spawned in other times and planes of existence. Many could be fought and slain only by magical weapons or by incantations read from dusty volumes or pieces of crumbling parchment. But Conan's taste had never run to spells and counterspells. He trusted his keen-edged sword more than all the magical mummery.

However, no demon from the darker haunts barred his way. He reached the tower without seeing a single sign of life among the shrubs and flowers.

Just then the clouds slid away from the moon. By the bright moonlight, Conan saw that the yellowish color of the tower was caused by an abundance of small golden coins set in plaster. Conan peered at those on a level with his eyes. None was familiar, and he suspected that it was the same with the rest. All had the look of great age. On some, the golden ridges of letters and cryptic signs had been worn away until nothing but a polished disk remained.

Conan knew that gold was considered a valuable auxiliary in making magic, especially in the form of coins from the ancient kingdoms. Here, thought Conan, were tokens from the long-dead realms of forgotten legendry, when priests and wizards ruled with awful terror, dragging maidens screaming to dark caverns where ghastly rituals were performed, or beheading thousands of prisoners in the public squares until rivers of bubbling blood filled the gutters.

Conan shivered. Much evil was concentrated here. Nevertheless, he tried the iron door.

The heavy slab of metal swung silently inward. Sword in hand, the Cimmerian entered, senses fine-whetted like those of a prowling tiger. By the faint light coming through the open door he could see two flights of stairs, one circling upward while the other lost itself in underground darkness.

Conan's keen nostrils picked up an alien smell from the stairs leading downwards. He suspected that this musky odor wafted up from a maze of caverns beneath the tower. The Cimmerian's eyes narrowed. Into his mind flitted the remembrance of similar odors in the haunted catacombs of the dead city of Pteion, in Stygia, where fearsome shapes wander by night. He shook his head as an angry lion shakes its mane.

Suddenly he was startled by words in a deep, resonant voice: "Welcome, Conan! Mount the stairs leading upward and follow the light!"

Glaring about, Conan could detect no clue to the origin of the voice. It seemed to come from everywhere, reverberating like the tones of a temple gong.

41

A glowing ball sprang into view in front of Conan, so suddenly that he took an instinctive step backwards. It hung in the air without visible support, shining brightly. By its light, Conan saw that he stood in a hall adorned with tapestries of ancient and curious design. One wall was covered with shelves on which stood oddly-shaped containers of stone, silver, gold, and jade. Some were set with gems, others were plain, and all were mingled helter-skelter.

The glowing globe moved slowly toward the stairs. Conon followed it without hesitation. One never knew the mind of a wizard, but Pelias at any rate seemed well-disposed towards the Cimmerian.

Not a creak sounded from the steps as Conan glided upwards, sword still in hand, though a little more relaxed than before. The steps ended on a landing barred by a copper-sheathed door with esoteric signs engraved in fanciful and involved patterns on its ruddy surface. Some of these Conan recognized from his wanderings as powerful magical symbols from the secret knowledge of ancient races. He scowled distrustfully. Then the door opened silently and the shimmering light went out.

Now there was no need of it. The room Conan entered was large and well-lighted. It was furnished with a mixture of flamboyant wall decorations and expensive works of art from many lands. A multitude of wall brackets held flaming tapers; soft rugs covered the floor.

In the center of the room stood an enormous, pillow-strewn divan. On this lay Pelias, a tall, lean, gray-haired man in scholar's robes. His eyes were dark and meditative, his head narrow and well-formed, his hands and feet small and trim. He had been studying, for empty spaces gaped in the huge bookcase and several volumes were scattered about the floor. Close by the divan, a large table was littered with parchment scrolls. At least they looked like parchment, though Conan knew that wizards preferred their mightiest spells to be written on cured human skin.

On the wall hung a mirror in a simple iron frame, contrasting with the luxury of the other furnishings. Conan was not surprised by the sybaritic atmosphere. Unlike most sorcerers, Pelias had never looked askance upon the pleasures of the flesh.

"Welcome, Conan!" cried the magician. "It has been nearly four years—" Then Pelias sprang up with narrowed eyes as Conan walked heavily forward, sheathing his sword. "You are wounded! And lately! You need a stronger draught than this wine. Wait!"

Pelias turned to an ornately-carved cupboard and opened one of its many small doors. From a recess he took a crystal flask, half full of a liquid of smoky violet hue. Into a wine cup he poured a good measure of the liquid and proferred it, saying:

"Drink this, my friend. It is made from the secret herbs of the Misty Isles and the lands beyond Kush. It will heal your wounds and ease your tired muscles."

Conan downed the draught with one mighty gulp. For a moment he grimaced. His veins seemed afire and his brain whirled and reeled. Then these feelings were replaced by sensations of well-being and content. A vast weight of weariness seemed lifted from his shoulders; he had not realized how fatigued his wounds and exertions had left him.

Pulling off his dented helmet, Conan felt his tingling scalp under the bandage. His hair was still matted with dried blood, but no wound could he find, not even a scar. His side and other wounded parts had stopped aching.

"Truly this is a magical brew, Pelias!" he said. "It is potent indeed. Apart from the rare ingredients, many potent incantations have been read over it to bring out the full powers of the recipe."

Conan grunted as he pulled off his mailshirt. "Would I had possessed it many a former time in my life!"

"Let us move on to the question of your errand. What brings you alone and in haste? I have not heard of any strife or great wars in the northwest, in which you might need my aid."

"Were it only straightforward war, I would never ask magical help," growled Conan. "But I find myself pitted against dark and unknown powers. I need clues to lead me to where I can smite my foe."

In swift, short sentences he told of the fateful night in Tarantia.

For a long time Pelias brooded with his chin in his hands. His eyes were closed, and some might have thought him asleep. Conan, however, knew that the wizard's brain was working with abnormal speed and keenness behind that deceptive mask. Slowly Pelias' eyes opened. He spoke.

"A demon of the darkest realms beyond the Mountains of the Night has stolen your spouse. I know how to summon one, but I thought I shared that knowledge with no one else in the West."

"Then fetch this fiend and we'll wring the truth out of him!"

"Not so fast, my hot-headed friend! Do not rush headlong into unknown dangers! It is clear that this demon has been summoned by a sorcerer with powers superior to those of ordinary magicians. Should we drag the fiend hither with spells and incantations, we should have both him and his master to cope with, and that might be too much for us. No; I know a better way. The Mirror of Lazbekri shall give us the answer!"

44

He rose. Again opening the cupboard, he brought out a dully gleaming cup whose rim was inscribed with curious symbols. Conan, who had gained a smattering of many written languages in his wanderings, did not recognize the script.

From a small jar the wizard poured a measure of red powder into the cup. Then he placed the cup on a low ebony table beneath the plain, iron-framed mirror. He threw back the folds of silk from his arm and made a cryptic gesture.

Blue smoke began to spiral up from the cup. It thickened until its billowing clouds filled the room. Conan could but dimly discern the motionless form of the wizard, petrified in trance during his concentration.

For an age, it seemed, nothing happened. Conan began to shift his weight with impatience when he heard Pelias' whisper:

"The sorcerer's defenses are strong, Conan. I cannot pierce them. Who is your tutelary deity?"

"It would be Crom, the grim god of the Cimmerians," muttered Conan, "though I have had naught to do with gods for many years. I leave them alone and they leave me alone."

"Well, pray to your Crom for help. We need it."

Conan closed his eyes and, for the first time in decades, prayed: "O Father Crom, who breathes power to strive and slay into a man's soul at birth, help your son against the demon that has stolen his mate . . ."

And into his brain he thought he heard the cold words come: "Long have you forsaken me, O Conan. But you are my true son for all that, in your striving and enduring and conquering. Look!"

Conan opened his eyes. The smoke had begun to thin. The Cimmerian saw that the mirror did not, as one might expect, show the reflection of Pelias; indeed, it showed no reflection at all. Its surface was a deep gray, as if this were a window to forbidden dimensions. In a low monotone, Pelias chanted an incantation in a tongue that Conan recognized as the secret language used by the priests of Stygia in their clandestine rituals in dark-walled Khemi.

Slowly, so slowly that it was not immediately noticeable, a picture took form in the mirror. At first it was blurred and uncertain; then swiftly it cleared and sharpened. In a bare, stone-walled room, a cowled and robed figure sat at a low table, a scroll in his hands.

The picture grew as if the point of vantage of the watchers moved nearer and nearer the hooded one. Suddenly the figure in the mirror threw up its head and looked full into their faces. The hood fell back from the yellow, hairless pate; the slitted, oblique eyes gazed coldly into theirs. The thin, colorless lips parted in a ghastly grin. The yellow one's right hand plunged into the folds of his robe and came out again holding a shining ball. The man made a motion as if to throw it—and then Conan exploded into lightning action.

A whistling slash of his heavy sword, held in readiness against the unknown perils of the mirror, sheared the frame in two and shattered the reflecting surface into thousands of tinkling splinters.

Pelias gave a start and shook himself like a man awakening. He said:

"By Ishtar, Conan, you saved us both! That shining thing was as deadly as a nest of cobras. Had he managed to throw it into this room, we should have been torn to bits in a holocaust that might have destroyed half the city. I was spellbound by the necessary concentration and could do nothing."

"The devil with that," grunted Conan, who had never learned to accept praise graciously. "Now, what did all this mean? I saw the man was a Khittan. What has he to do with my quest?"

Pelias' somber eyes rested upon the huge Cimmerian as his answer came from stiff lips. "My friend, these matters are deeper than I thought. The fate of the world may rest upon you."

The sorcerer paused, swilling a draught of wine. Leaning back on his cushions, he continued. Outside, the night was black and still.

"The magicians of the West have long been aware that the effects of certain spells have been weakened or nullified. This condition has been growing more marked in recent years. During the past few months I have buried myself in research, prying for the cause of this phenomenon. And I have found it.

"We are entering a new era. Enlightenment and reason are spreading among the peoples of the West. Aquilonia stands as a bulwark among the nations, strengthening its imperial powers by the naked, elemental force of the healthy barbarian mind. You have rejuvenated the nation, and similar forces are at work in other realms. The bonds of black magic are strained and broken by new factors brought in by the changed conditions. The far-flung web of intrigue and evil spun by the black forces is fraying.

"Some of the most evil spells would now hardly succeed at all in the Western realms. This resistance of civilization to the magic of darkness is concentrated in the barbarian king of Aquilonia. You have long been the center of mighty happenings, and the gods look favorably upon you. And so things will continue to change until, with another turn of the cosmic wheel, enlightenment shall perish and magic shall rise again to power in a new cycle.

"I grow old, I who am already older than men reckon. Nowadays I use my vast knowledge only to furnish a life of ease and comfort and to pursue my scholarly researches. I do not live as an ascetic in ragged robes, summoning red-eyed beings with slavering jaws and ripping claws to wreak havoc among innocent human beings.

"But there is one who has long thirsted for absolute power over the world and all that dwell therein. He has become obsessed by the idea. Years ago he began to lay the groundwork for the gigantic, cataclysmal acts of dark necromancy that should rock the earth to its core and enslave its inhabitants.

"This I learned through my unearthly spies: When, one night, he cut out the living heart of a maiden on an altar in a deserted temple by moonlight and mumbled a terrible incantation over it, he failed to get the results he sought. He was dumbfounded; this was his first attempt upon the western countries.

"His failure roused him to insensate rage. For days and nights without end he labored to find who opposed him, and at last he succeeded. *You* are his main obstacle.

"This dark plan, whose outlines I now grasp, is worthy of his twisted genius. By stealing your spouse, he forces you to go after her. He is sure you will be slain by foes along the way or slaughtered by the strange and unknown peoples that dwell east of the Himelian Mountains. Should you by some feat of prowess or stroke of luck reach his haunts, he counts on slaying you himself by his diabolical powers.

"After that, the road to conquest will be open to him, for the resistance forged here in the West is too young yet to stand without its backbone—Conan, the king of Aquilonia!"

Dryness rasped Pelias' throat; he sipped the wine.

"As you know, I am accounted one of the mightiest magicians of the West, even though I nowadays seldom use my full powers. But should I be pitted against him of whom I speak, I should not have the chance of a ewe in a pool of crocodiles. The sorcerers of the East are mightier than those of the West, and he is the mightiest of all. He is Yah Chieng of Paikang, in Khitai."

Conan pondered this information with somber eyes and immobile features. At last the deep tones of his voice resounded.

"By Crom, Pelias, there rests more upon my shoulders than I could ever fathom, if what you've said is true. But I care not for the fate of the world, if I can only get my Zenobia back!"

"Ah, my friend, the fate of you, of your queen, and of the world are fast entwined. Mighty events are upon us; the destinies of uncounted ages to come will soon be decided. This is Yah Chieng's supreme bid for power. He is sure of success, or the crawling snake would not have dared attempt it. This kidnaping is but a trick to lure you from the West, which you are guarding against evil eastern sorcery. Think, man, and compare! Which is the more important: a single woman or the fate of millions?"

"The devil with that, Pelias!" roared Conan. "D'you think I would let my woman be torn from my side and then stay at home because I am some sort of wizard's jinx? May the demons of Shaggali eat the marrow of my bones if I care one copper's worth for kingship, power, lands, or riches! I want my woman back, and I'll have her if I must carve my way through a hundred thousand swordsmen to reach that bald-pated scoundrel!"

Pelias shrugged. He realized that the savage promptings that guided the barbarian's actions would not be affected by his disclosure of the deeper causes of the recent events. The only world Conan really cared about was the one that now surrounded him with red-blooded life. He had little concern for the future. Pelias said:

"Alas, the Fates have already spun their web, and I cannot change it. Now listen. Paikang, in Khitai, is your goal. There Yah Chieng lives in his purple tower, guarded by two hundred giant Khitan sabermen, the most skilled in the East. He has usurped the power of the rightful rulers, and he governs with flail and whip. Beware his black arts. By a wave of his hand he can blot an army from the earth. I know not if I can help you, but I will try. Come with me."

The lean wizard rose and went to a small, gold-inlaid secretary-table made of some strange wood. There was an oddness about its looks, as if the craft that had fashioned it was not of human origin. Conan was a little mystified. In all his wanderings he had never seen furniture in this style.

Pelias pressed a projection hidden among the carvings of one leg of the table. A small drawer shot out, and the wizard picked an object from it. It was a ring. Strangely wrought, it did not shine with the fire of gold, nor with the icy gleam of silver, nor yet with the rich red of copper. Its dull-blue lustre was not like that of any known metal. All along its band were hieroglyphs of ancient origin. Bending to peer, Conan recognized forbidden symbols found only on the altar friezes of the secret temples of certain inhuman gods worshiped in Stygia.

The seal, also, was strangely fashioned. It was of rhombic shape, with the upper and lower points long and sharp. A careless man could easily prick himself with it.

Pelias gazed at the ring for a moment. Its strange blue gleam was like a sword of icy flame in the room. The Cimmerian, with his fine-whetted senses, could feel the power emanating from the thing. Then the wizard straightened and brushed back a grizzled lock from his forehead.

"Many moons have passed since I won this ring," he intoned. "For days and nights without cease I fought its owner, a powerful sorcerer of Luxur. The fury of the dark powers we unleashed might have devastated the land had not our spells and counter-spells canceled each other. With brain whirling and senses reeling, I strove with him through eons of black time. When I felt I could not continue much longer, he suddenly gave up. He changed his form to that of a hawk and tried to flee. My strength resurged within me: I transformed myself into an eagle, swooped upon him, and tore him to shreds. Ha! Those were the days when I was young and gloried in my powers!

"Now, my friend, I want you to wear this ring. It will be a powerful aid on your journey. Have you heard of Rakhamon?"

Conan nodded. The southern countries were rife with legends of the past, but still the name of that dread sorcerer was whispered with caution, though a full century and a half had passed since his end. Hyrkanian invaders had sacked and burned his city while he lay helpless in the stupor induced by the black lotus.

Many adepts in magic had sought for his secret books, said to be written on the dried skins of maidens flayed alive, but none had found them. If this ring was

51

a relic of Rakhamon's possessions, it must be powerful indeed.

"Aye, this is the ring of Rakhamon," said Pelias gravely. "Some of the unnatural beings summoned from the darker realms could not, once called, be controlled by the usual protective spells. Therefore he fashioned this ring of a metal he found in the stone of a fallen star during his travels in the icy North. He invested the ring with unimaginable powers by secret and nameless rituals, in which blood was spilled in profusion and screaming souls were condemned to the deepest and darkest hell. The wearer of this ring can stand against any beast summoned by magical arts, that much I know.

"As to its detailed use, there is no clue. Probably the knowledge perished with the secret manuscripts. Take it, Conan! This is all I can aid you with. No other spells I know can avail against the evil power of Yah Chieng."

Conan took the proffered ornament. At first it seemed too small for his massive fingers, but as he tried it on the middle finger of his left hand it slid lightly on. It seemed to have a life of its own; it fitted as if made to order. The Cimmerian shrugged. Decades of experience had made him casual about the pretensions of magical things. The bauble might work, and if not, no harm would come of it. At least, Pelias' intentions were good.

"To the devil with all this talk," said the barbarian. "I have a long journey before me. A loaf, a joint of meat, and a skin of wine, and I am for bed. Could you spare me a cot for the night?"

"Any sort of bed you desire, my friend. My servants will fetch food and tend your horse." Pelias clapped his hands.

"That reminds me," said Conan, yawning. "I must sacrifice a bullock to Crom ere I set forth tomorrow. Say nothing of it, for, if they knew, people would say: Conan grows old; he is getting religious in his dotage!"

3. Vengeance From the Desert

THE SUN GLINTED on spired helmets and whetted spearheads. Spurs jingled and bright silks flashed as three armored riders breasted the long slope of a great sand dune in the wide desert that formed the southwestern marches of Turan. Red turbans were wound about their helmets; sashes of the same color girdled their waists. White silken shirts, baggy trousers thrust into short black boots, and sleeveless, silvered mailshirts completed their apparel. Curved swords hung at their hips. Upright from the holders that hung from the saddles of two of them rose the ten-foot Turanian lances. The remaining one bore, slung from his saddle, a thick, double-curved bow in a bow case and a score and a half of arrows in a lacquered leathern quiver.

Accompanying them was a fourth figure, bound by both wrists to a rope held by the bowman. Deep gashes in the sand told of this prisoner's inability to keep up with his mounted captors. He wore the white khalat of the desert Zuagir, though the garment was dirty and torn to shreds. His lean, dark visage was hollow-cheeked, but implacable hatred lurked in his red-rimmed eyes. He stumbled panting up the slope without a sound of pain or protest.

The Turanian soldiers, separated from the rest of their troop by a two-day sandstorm, were seeking their way back to Fort Wakla, a Turanian outpost deep in the Zuagir desert country. Yesterday they had met the Zuagir. His horse had tumbled under him with an arrow through its heart, and he had been laid senseless on the sand by a blow from a spear butt. The commander of Fort Wakla had lately begun an intense campaign against the desert tribes, who had harried Kuranian caravans overly much of late. Having taken the Zuagir prisoner, the horsemen were bringing him back to the fort to be bled of knowledge before being hanged.

At the top of the dune, the little troop paused to rest. Waterskins were lifted to parched mouths, while the ragged prisoner crawled up on all fours, almost done in. Sand dunes stretched as far as the eye could see. As practiced warriors, the Turanians used the pause to let their hawklike eyes sweep the horizon and the surface of the sands. Nothing could be seen save endless, rolling yellow plain.

The tallest of the three, the man with the bow and the prisoner's rope, suddenly stiffened. Shading his dark eyes, he bent forward to get a better view. On the top of a dune a mile away, he had sighted a lone horseman riding at a gallop. The dune had hidden him as they came to their point of vantage, but now the stranger was flying down the near side in a flurry of sand. The leader turned to his fellows.

"By the alabaster hips of Yenagra!" he said, "we have caught another desert rat! Be ready; we will kill this one and take his head on a lance tip back to the fort."

Knowing there would be no trouble to recover the Zuagir after the fight, he dropped the rope. He spurred his mount down the slope towards the point in the wide valley of sand, where he counted on intercepting the stranger, and in one smooth motion drew the powerful bow from its case and nocked an arrow. His fellow troopers followed with spears poised and slitted eyes agleam, yelping like hounds closing for the kill.

At three hundred paces, the bowman drew and loosed at full gallop with the effortless horsemanship of a Turanian cavalryman. But the shaft did not strike home. Like lightning his intended victim flung his horse aside with a mighty effort that almost threw the steed. With a swift gesture, the stranger shook off the folds of his khalat.

The Hyrkanians halted in consternation. There appeared before them not the half-starved form of a desert man, armed only with knife and javelin, but a powerful western warrior in sturdy mail and steel helmet, equipped with a long sword and a dagger. The sword flashed like a flame in the sunlight as the rider whipped it out. The Turanian leader's narrow eyes widened with astonishment.

"You dare return to Turan, barbarian scoundrel!" he cried. For the Turanian was Hamar Kur, who had been amir of a troop of horse that Conan, as a leader of the *kozaki*, had routed years before by an ambush on the Yelba River. Hamar Kur was demoted to common trooper in the frontier guards in consequence and ever since had burned for vengeance. Drawing his saber, he shouted:

"At him, men! It is Conan the *kozak!* Slay him, and the king will fill your helmets with gold!"

The Turanian riders hesitated, awed by the memory of gory and terrible legends associated with that name. Tales told how this man, with two pirate galleys, had sacked and burned the fortified seaport of Khawarizm and then broken through six of the king's war galleys that had come to trap him, leaving three foundering and the others' decks awash with blood. They told how he, with a band of Zuagir tribesmen, had harried the outflung Imperial posts in the south until the border had to be drawn back. They told how the savage kozak hordes under his command had stormed the walled city of Khorosun, slaying and burning.

Conan made full use of his enemies' moment of indecision. Spurring his big horse, he thundered upon them like a one-man avalanche, his sword flashing in circles. Hamar Kur's mount reared wildly before this crashing charge and was cast to the ground. Its rider was spilled from the saddle.

The two other soldiers couched their lances and spurred fiercely, but lacked time to gain enough speed to make their charge effective. With the fury of a thunderstorm Conan was upon them, smiting right and left. The head of one man leaped from its trunk on a fount of blood. The next instant, Conan's blade shattered the other's lance. The Turanian caught the following blow on his shield but was hurled from his saddle by sheer impact.

Hamar Kur had regained his feet. Skilled in combat against horsemen, he ran to where the slain trooper had dropped his lance. Then he ran swiftly up and thrust the shaft of the weapon between the legs of Conan's horse. He cast himself aside at the last moment to avoid the barbarian's terrible sword.

The desert sands clouded the sky as Conan and his mount crashed to the ground together. With the practiced ease of the hardened mercenary, the Cimmerian threw himself clear. He rose, sword still in hand. With cold blue eyes slitted he watched his two surviving enemies slink towards him, one from either side. Their tactics were obvious: to catch him between them so that one could strike him down from the rear.

With tigerish swiftness, he charged the soldier to the right. He knew he risked a scimitar in the back from Hamar Kur, but it was never his way to await the

57

foe's attack. The Turanian tried to parry the crashing blow, but to no avail. Splintering the curled blade with its terrible force, the Cimmerian's sword smashed helmet and skull like a ripe orange.

Conan wheeled like a panther in the nick of time. He just managed to catch Hamar Kur's whistling blow on his sword hilt. There was a momentary exchange of cuts and parries as the straight blade of the West and the curved blade of the East whirled about each other in a coruscating dance of death. Then a quick thrust from Conan pierced his enemy's breast. The point drove through the fine Turanian mail and on through the ex-amir's body. Hamar gave a ghastly scream and fell heavily. Conan braced his legs to tear his dripping blade free.

The Cimmerian wiped his sword on his enemy's sash and looked swiftly around. He had heard a sound from behind, and his senses and temper were on edge. He waited warily as a tattered figure half slid and half rolled down the slope almost to his feet. It was the Zuagir. Rising on shaky legs, he spat upon the prostrate form of Hamar Kur. Then he turned his burning eyes on Conan. As he took in the gigantic figure in worn mail, the rage and fury in his eyes gave way to recognition and joy. Lifting his bound hands, he cried:

"Praise be to Kemosh, for he has answered my prayers and sent these dogs to the floors of Hell! And more, he has brought back the great warlord who led us to plunder long ago! I greet you, Hawk of the Desert! There will be feasting and dancing in the villages! The Turanian dogs will cower in their towers as the cry goes forth from the desert: 'Yamad al-Aphta has returned!'"

Conan shrugged his broad shoulders and thrust his

sword back into the scabbard. His horse had risen from its fall, and Conan unslung his waterskin and pack from the saddle.

"Here, wolf," he grunted, "you look a little the worse for wear. Have a draught, but take care you are not overfilled." Conan brought out bread and dried meat and shared them with the Zuagir. "Now tell me: What is afoot in the desert? How did you fall into the hands of the Hyrkanians?"

The nomad answered between gulps and champings: "I am Yar Allal of the Duali tribe. I was riding in haste and alone for our camp when these dogs caught me. They shot my horse from under me and stunned me with a blow on the head. They were bringing me back to Fort Wakla for questioning and death."

"Whence your hurry?" asked Conan. "And why alone? These hills swarm with Turanian patrols."

The voice of the Zuagir took on a burning edge as he answered. "A terrible misfortune has struck our tribe. Listen, my lord. For days we lay in wait in the ruins of the Gharat temple, fifty miles to the south. Word had come that a rich caravan was approaching from the west, bringing the wealth and person of the lady Thanara."

"Who's that?"

"A *yedka* of Maypur, famed for her beauty and riches. Furthermore she is high in the favor of King Yezdigerd. Could we but capture her, a fabulous ransom would be ours as well as the spoils from the camel train.

"We lay there with knives whetted and bows newly strung until we thought the dogs of traders would never come. And then, one day, we heard the camels' bells in the distance. The long line of men, beasts, and wagons came into view.

"We waited until they were almost upon us. Uttering our war cry, we swept down upon them. We expected an easy conquest of the merchants and their retainers. Then, suddenly, the merchants and servants threw aside their khalats. Instead of timid civilians, mailed lancers in the white turbans of the Imperial Guard rushed against us!

"There must have been a hundred of them hidden in the wains. They rode through our ranks like reapers mowing down a field of wheat. Half of us perished in the first attack. The rest were riven apart and scattered into small bands. We fought mightily against the odds, and many a Turanian plunged to earth with a Duali spear through his throat or a curved knife in his guts.

"But our courage was of no avail as the steel-clad ranks closed in upon us. I saw my brother felled by a stroke from the amir's scimitar. Then Yin Allal, my father, caught a blow on the head that knocked him stunned from the saddle. I spurred my horse; smiting and thrusting I won through and away. They pursued me for hours, but their horses were wearier than mine and they gave it up. I was on my way to raise the tribe as I was caught. By now the caravan is safely within the walls of Fort Wakla. There will be rejoicing among the Turanians tonight; not for decades have they captured a Zuagir chief alive!"

"How know you he is alive?"

"In the last moment ere I raced off, I looked back and saw two of them carrying him back toward the carts. He was moving, though feebly."

Conan digested this tale. He well remembered Yin Allal, one of his staunchest supporters of old, when he, as war chief of three united Zuagir tribes, had led them in daring raids against the Turanians. Confronted by this new problem, he did not wish to leave an old friend unaided in the hands of his enemies. He sprang up, his blue eyes flashing with determination.

"Catch yourself a horse!" he snapped. "We ride for the Duali oasis at once. We shall be there by nightfall, and if my name is not forgotten I'll raise the tribes again. I will save my old friend. We'll pull those dogs' beards yet, by Crom!"

With a laugh he flung himself into the saddle. Gesturing to his companion to follow, he spurred his horse into a fierce gallop over the sands.

The oasis lay enfolded in the black arms of the desert night. Stars twinkled like gems on a dark mantel studded with diamonds; the fronds of the palms, now and then moving before the slight evening breeze, were silvered by the cold moonlight. In the shadow of the foliage were strewn a profusion of tents—a large Zuagir camp.

Earlier in the day, this had been a quiet place. The desert sun poured its golden rays upon the camel's-hair dwellings. Veiled women went about their primitive duties, fetching water from the well and broiling strips of meat over the campfires. Snores and snuffles sounded from the nomadic abodes as the tribesmen took their siesta.

Now the Duali oasis was a center of frantic activity. In the middle rose a tent whose size indicated its importance. From this tent, now and then, a lean desert hawk emerged. The Zuagir would hurry with flapping khalat to his horse, spring into the saddle, and urge the mount into a mad race out over the desert. Others returned from their missions, flinging themselves from foam-flecked steeds to hasten toward the big central tent. Zuagirs from the neighboring tribes of the Kharoya and Qirlata had been pouring in all day. Now the area covered by dun-colored tents was thrice as large as the day before. Conversations were whispered behind the door flaps; men went to and fro on urgent errands. There was an orderly bustle such as is seldom seen in a desert camp.

The hearts of the robed and bearded chiefs in the central tent swelled with pride and affection. The huge figure in worn mail, seated in the place of honor, had become the center of legendry and hero worship since the day long ago when he had arrived among them. He united their bickering clans and led them in raids so daring, bloody, and rewarding that tales of them were still told around the campfires. Their superstitious minds regarded the return of the big Cimmerian as a good omen. This opinion was strengthened by having occurred at the same time that their raiding party had been nearly wiped out and one of their mightiest chiefs captured.

Petty inter-tribal quarrels were swept away by the return of the Hawk of the Desert. Savage expectation was mirrored in their dark eyes as Conan lectured them.

"The fort is impregnable to a straight assault," he said bluntly. "We have no ballistae or other siege engines to reduce it by force. It is well provisioned, like all these Turanian outposts, and might hold out for a year. Moreover, a determined sally by their seasoned squadrons would scatter our irregular ranks. Our chance is to come to grips with them inside the walls, where cavalry tactics cannot be used and we have the advantage of numbers. Trickery must be used.

"Let us equip a caravan train from the loot stored here in this oasis. Fifty of us, garbed as merchants, slaves, retainers, and camel drivers shall take the caravan to the fort, as if we were on the road to Kherdpur. At the twelfth hour we shall cut down the guards at the gate, open up, and let in the horde. Our main goals are the barracks, the officers' quarters, and the governor's palace. We shall pillage, burn sack, and slay until the streets run red with Turanian blood!"

The Cimmerian rose, hitching at his scabbard. "To work, desert dogs! Before sunrise, I want such a camel train as would make any Zuagir's mouth water!"

Camel bells tinkled. The feet of men and beasts raised clouds of dust as the long line passed through the gate of Fort Wakla. At the gate, the lean merchant in the lead declared: "Lord, I am Zebah, a Shemite of Anakia. I have come up from Yukkub to barter my goods in Kherdpur."

"Who is this?" asked the gate captain, pointing to a huge man wrapped in a capacious khalat. His kaffia hid the lower part of his face, so that only his piercing blue eyes could be seen.

"This is my personal servant and boydguard," declared the leader, "a Stygian. The others are hired guards, camel drivers, and slaves. By Ashtoreth, it is good to be safely within walls again! I had feared attacks from the Zuagir bands. My men are well armed, as the noble captain can see. But the gods protected us, so none of those stinking vermin of the desert assailed us."

The captain of the watch grinned. "Your precautions were wasted, my man. Just now a woman could ride alone and unmolested along the caravan trail. Yesterday a squadron of the Imperial Guards smashed a host of the desert rats and captured their chieftain. We think only one of the dogs got away."

"Ah!" said the Shemite. "That is indeed glorious news."

"All in the day's work. But at least this show of

63

force should stop the raids for a while. Veziz Shah has ordered us to slay any Zuagir, man, woman, or child, caught by our patrols. By the time you return to Yukkub, you will be able to travel the length and breadth of the Zuagir desert without fear."

"I will burn an offering to Bel as a measure of my gratitude," said the merchant, as the last of the camels shambled through the gate. Four guardsmen closed the gate; its ironclad valves swung creakingly shut on hinges as thick as a man's leg. The massive bolt bars clanged into their cradles.

The fort was really a small city. A high, crenelated wall of stone girded the mass of buildings with parapets and battlements. Watchful bowmen ranged the breastworks. The space within was roomy, and merchants and thieves found their means of support in the profusion of buildings. Isolated as it was, Fort Wakla must contain within itself the means of civilized living, with drinking shops and gambling houses to keep the garrison happy.

At the spacious market place in the center, mailed soldiers in spired helmets and robed merchants with exotic wares and veiled women milled about. The space resounded with the cries of hawkers and auctioneers. To one side rose the mighty citadel where the governor lived, a fortress in itself with gray stone walls, narrow windows, and heavy copper doors. Those who had been inside, however, averred that the interior belied the grimness of the outside. It was heaped with art treasures, fitted with comfortable furniture, and stocked with fine wines and viands.

Evening had come. The sky darkened swiftly, and here and there candles and lamps illuminated the windows. Sweating taverners bore wine casks from their cellars for the evening rush of customers. Gamblers rolled dice with practiced twists and turns. The colorful night life of a Hyrkanian city was beginning.

In the quarters by the western wall, reserved for visiting caravans, arguments raged around the campfires of Conan's band. Nearly all advocated staying there in safety, unsuspected, until the appointed hour had come. But Conan was of another mind. With a good two-hours to spare, he meant to find out as much as he could about the disposition of the enemy. The quarters of the officers and common soldiers he had already located, close by the main gate, but he did not know the number of the troops quartered there.

"May the fiends cut off your tongues!" he rumbled. "I will do as I have said. In the tavern district there will be scores of drunken soldiers off duty. From one of them I shall get the information I want if I have to wring it from him like a sodden cloth!"

The iron determination of the Cimmerian swept aside the objections of his followers. He wrapped his khalat about him and strode away, hiding his face under the kaffia. There was no reason to upset their carefully laid plans by letting some Turanian with a good memory recognize him.

The fumes of sour wine, stale beer, and sweat struck Conan in the face as he entered the first drinking shop. The carousal was in full swing. Wenches hurried to and fro with jacks of foaming ale and flagons of wine, while painted hussies dawdled on the knees of half-drunken soldiers who emptied their wine cups and yelled for more. The interior was much like that of a western tavern, though the garb was more colorful.

Seeking out a small, secluded table in a darker corner, the big barbarian sat down upon a creaking chair and ordered a tankard of beer. Slaking his thirst in gulps, he looked around. A pair of drunken lancers were wrestling on the floor amid shrieks and titters from the women. Taut muscles rippled under their tawny, sweating skins. A game of dice was in progress at a neighboring table. Gleaming coins and flashing gems wandered from one side to the other across its rough-hewn and wine-spattered surface. The Cimmerian relaxed. Nervousness seldom assailed him, but his senses had been on edge as he entered the enemy's lair.

"What about a drink, you silent dullard?"

With a crash of overturned chairs, a giant man-at-arms pushed through the throng, leaving a train of furious curses in his wake. He flung himself down upon the unoccupied seat at Conan's table. His eyes were glassily belligerent, and his gilded mail and silken sash were splashed with wine from his cup.

Conan's eyes narrowed. The man wore the scarlet mantle and white turban of the Imperial Guards. The turban sported a peacock feather, the emblem of a captain of these elite troops. No doubt he belonged to that detachment that routed the Zuagirs and took Yin Allal prisoner. In fact he might have commanded that company. Here was an opportunity sent by the gods if Conan could but use it.

With a show of bluff intimacy, the big Cimmerian leaned forward, his face still hidden in the shadow of his kaffia. "Do not wonder that I find this place dull. I came in only to slake my thirst." He gave the soldier a friendly punch in the shoulder. "I'm on my way to a pleasure house where the women are so fair and skilled as to rival the courtezans of Shadizar!"

The captain hiccuped, shook his head, and focussed his eyes with an effort. "Huh? Women? Good idea. Who are you, anyway?"

"Hotep of Khemi, bodyguard to the merchant Zebah. Come along with me, man! A visit to this place will surfeit you for a month."

Conan was not an expert dissembler. His performance would have aroused the suspicion of a shrewd and sober man. However, the drunken stupor of the Turanian left room for nothing but his most primitive instincts. Breathing hard with aroused lust, he leaned forward with a loud belch.

"Lead me there, man! I have wandered too long over the cursed desert without a woman."

"Were you with the party that ambushed the Zuagirs?"

"With them? I commanded them!"

"Good for you!"

"Aye; that was a noble fight. But the only wench in the caravan was the *yedka* Thanara, may the gods smite her haughty body with boils!"

"She refused you?"

"Worse! She slapped me when I tried to kiss her in her tent!"

"The insolence of her!" said Conan.

"Nor was that all. Would you believe it, she threatened to have me flayed in the great square at Agrapur if I did not behave? Me, Ardashir of Akif! Behave myself! As if any red-blooded man could control himself when casting his eyes upon her!"

"It is shameful, how women treat us."

"Enough of that. Lead me to your pleasure house, Stygian. I need forgetfulness and surcease."

Rising unsteadily, the Turanian pushed through the throng. Conan followed. In the street, the cool night air was like a slap in the face with a wet cloth. The captain sobered visibly as he walked. Suddenly curious, he peered at the half-hidden face of his companion, who hurried silently along at his side.

"Ho," he said, "Wait a moment, my fleet-footed

friend! You have not described the whereabouts of this magical house of women, of which I have never heard though I know Wakla well. Let's have a look under your headsheet—"

Ardashir's speech was cut short by a powerful hand on his throat. Corded muscles of unimaginable strength held him as in a giant vice. Normally accounted the strongest man in his company, he was, in his unsteady condition, helpless against the suddenness of the assault and the gorillalike power of the Cimmerian.

He was swiftly dragged into a dark lane, struggling for breath and clawing at the hands that throttled him. When he was almost unconscious, he was swiftly trussed with his own sash. Roughly turned over on his back, he felt the burning eyes of his captor upon him as the barbarian spoke heavily accented Hyrkanian in a sibilant whisper:

"You asked my name, eastern dog! Have you heard of Conan, called Yamad al-Aphta by the Zuagirs? Chief of the *kozaki* and the Vilayet pirates?"

The Turanian could do no more than make a choking sound in his bruised throat. Conan continued: "I have returned from the West, and now I will have information from you if I have to burn out your eyes or skin the soles of your feet to get it!"

Though a tough and courageous man, Ardashir was paralyzed with shock. Normal enemies, such as Zaugir bands, Kshatriya legions, or the defending troops of invaded western nations he had faced with the fatalistic hardihood of the seasoned warrior. But this barbarian giant, kneeling over him with poised dagger, was regarded with superstitious dread by the Turanians. The saga of his daring exploits had invested him with magical powers in their eyes, until his name was spoken like that of a mythical ogre.

Ardashir knew that the barbarian's threats were not idle. Conan would carry out the most bestial acts of torture without compunction to gain his own ends. Yet it was not the fear of torture but rather the numbing realization of the identity of his captor that loosed Ardashir's tongue.

By prodding a little with his dagger now and then, Conan gathered his news. The regular garrison of twelve hundred horse was quartered in the barracks by the main gate, while the hundred men of the Imperial Guard were spread over the city in temporary quarters. The desert chieftain was chained in the dungeon beneath the governor's tower. The lady Thanara was also quartered in the tower. The strength of the guards at the gates the captain did not know.

Conan pondered the situation. He knew that the barracks formed a square with a single exit. He had over two thousand determined nomads at his disposal. But using his new-found knowledge effectively, he counted on gaining victory.

A glance at the moon told him the twelfth hour was near. It was time to hurry. He tested the bonds of his captive, gagged him with his own turban, dragged him farther into the lane, and left him there, glaring and straining.

"I must be growing soft," Conan said to himself. "Time was when I should have cut the cur's throat after questioning him. But the Zuagirs will no doubt take care of that when they find him."

Faint, rapid drum beats filled the luxurious apartment on the second floor of the governor's palace, where Thanara of Maypur lounged on a silken divan, nibbling fruit from a low table that stood on the thick rug in front of her couch. Her sheerly transparent gown revealed her seductive charms, but the man in the room paid scant attention to these.

This man was a small, bandy-legged, mud-colored fellow, clad in skins and furs. His flat, wrinkled, monkeylike face was painted with stripes and circles of red and black. His long black hair was gathered in greasy braids, and a necklace of human teeth encircled his neck. A powerful stench of sweat-soaked leather and unwashed human hide rose from him. He was a Wigur, one of those fierce and barbarous nomads from the far northeast beyond the Sea of Vilayet.

The little man sat cross-legged on the floor and stared at the thin curl of smoke that rose from a brazier on a tripod in front of him. The wavering blue column soared up from its source for two feet, then rippled and curled up on itself in interwoven arabesques. All the while the man kept up a swift tapping of his finger tips against a small drum, less than a foot across, which he held in his other hand.

At last the staccato tapping stopped.

"What see you, Tatur?" asked the *yedka*.

"He comes," said the shaman in a high singsong voice. "He whom you seek is near."

"How can he be?" said the lady Thanara sharply. "Veziz Shah keeps a sharp watch, and no such conspicuous rogue could gain admittance."

"Nevertheless, he approaches," whined Tatur. "The spirits do not lie. Unless you flee, he will soon confront you."

"He must have entered Wakla in disguise," mused Thanara. "If he comes upon me, what shall I do? Will your master, he who is not to be named, give me some means to cope with him?" There was a note of panic in her voice, and her hand sought her shapely throat.

"It is the will of him who shall not be named that you should succeed in your mission," intoned the Wigur. He fumbled inside his sheepskin coat and brought out a small purple phial.

"A drop of this in his wine," he said, "will render him like one dead for three days."

"That is good. But the barbarian is wary. His suspicions are aroused in the wink of an eye, as we learned at Khanyria. Suppose he detects the drug and refuses to drink?"

Tartur brought out another object: a small pouch of soft leather. "In that case, this will lay him low if he breathes it."

"What is it?"

"Pollen of the yellow lotus of Khitai. Use it only as a last resort. For, should a breath of air blow it back upon you, you too will be cast into a swoon. And too deep a breath of it can kill."

"That is good, but not enough. If your master really expects me to confront the Cimmerian, he should furnish me with a last-minute means of escape if I am trapped. Others may underestimate the Cimmerian, but not I. And your master can do it, and he owes it to me for past services."

A faint smile creased Tatur's wrinkled features. "He who is not to be named said truly you are a sharp bargainer. Here." He brought out an object like a translucent egg. "Break this in your hour of need, and help will come to you from other dimensions."

Thanara examined the three objects. "Good," she said at last. "Ride to Aghrapur and tell the king I await Conan here. If all goes well, he shall have his enemy. If not, he will need a new agent. Haste and farewell!"

71

A few minutes later, Tatur the shaman, astride a small, shaggy Hyrkanian pony, jogged off into the night across the sands at a tireless canter.

The night was cool and quiet. The captain of the watch at the main gate stretched and yawned. From the small guardhouse in the square before the gate, he could see two bowmen patrolling the parapet over the big twin doors. The pair of spearmen at the pillars flanking the entrance stood erect and still, the moonlight reflected by their polished mail shirts and spired helmets. No need to fear anything; a stroke on the gong at his side would bring a company on the double from the barracks. Nevertheless, the governor had ordered the guards doubled and their vigilance increased.

The officer wondered. Did Veziz Shah really fear an attack on the fort on account of the captured Zuagir chief? Let the desert rats come! They would smash their heads aginst the walls while the archers riddled them with arrows. The governor must be getting old and prone to nightmares. Let him rest. He, Akeb Man, was in charge!

The moon was obscured by clouds. Akeb Man blinked and peered. What had happened? It seemed as if the two archers on the wall had sat down for a moment. Now, however, they had risen again and resumed their measured pacing. Better investigate these lazy devils. He would give them three hours' drill in the desert sun if they had tried to shirk their duty.

Rising, he gazed out again before opening the door. At that instant the moonlight returned in full force. A shocking sight met his eyes. Instead of spired helmets and mantles, the archers wore banded kaffias and khalats.

Zuagirs!

How they had gotten in, only the devils knew. Akeb Man snatched at the hammer that hung beside the gong to strike the alarm.

The door of the guardhouse burst in with a crash and fell in a cloud of splinters and dust. Akeb Man wheeled and snatched at his scimitar, but the sight of the man confronting him made him pause in astonishment. No white-clad desert raider was he, but a giant western warrior in black mesh-mail, naked sword in hand.

With a cry of fear and rage, the Turanian lashed out with a low disemboweling thrust. With the swiftness of lightning, the mailed giant avoided the blade and brought his own long straight sword down in a whistling blow. Blood spurted like a fountain as Akeb Man sank to the floor, cloven to the breastbone.

Conan wasted no time in gloating. Any moment now, an inquisitive guardsman might poke his head through a barracks window or a belated citizen might come wandering by. The big iron-sheathed doors were now opening, and through them poured a swift and silent-footed stream of white-robed nomads.

Swiftly, Conan issued his orders. His tones were low, but the words carried to the ears of all.

"Two men with torches, set the barracks afire. Three hundred archers with plenty of arrows place themselves to mow down the soldiers as they pour out. The rest of you hit the fort with torch and sword. Burn and slay, and take any spoils and captives you want. Keep together. Do not break up into bands smaller than twenty. Thabit, bring your fifty with me. I am for the governor's palace."

With an imperious gesture, Conan dismissed his subchiefs and beckoned his fifty, who followed his iong strides at a dogtrot. Behind them, smoking torches lit the square as the arsonists slunk towards the guards-mens' lodgings. Other bands vanished in different directions. With the armed defenders of the fort wiped out by Conan's stratagem, there would be little opposition. The lean reavers licked their lips in anticipation of plunder and vengeance as they stalked along the silent streets, arrows nocked and knives and spears gleaming in the moonlight.

Conan led his men straight toward their goal. He intended to save Yin Allal first. Moreoever, he was intrigued by the tale of the beautiful *yedka*. Here, he thought, he might find a prize precious enough to satisfy his own taste. Beautiful women had always been one of his weaknesses, and his imagination had been fired by Ardashir's account. He increased his speed, watching the dimmed doorways and nighted lane mouths with smoldering eyes as he hurried past.

As they emerged upon the central square, Conan mouthed a barbaric oath. Four sentries paced in pairs before the copper door of the residence. He had counted on taking the governor by surprise, but that was no longer possible. Swinging his great sword, he raced across the flagstones of the market place. Such was his speed that one of the spearmen was down with his side caved in before the others collected their shattered wits. Conan's followers were twenty yards behind, unable to match the Cimmerian's terrific speed.

Two spearmen thrust their weapons against his broad breast, while the third put a horn to his lips and sent forth a bellowing signal. This was cut short by a well-aimed Zuagir arrow, which pierced the trumpeter's brain. The horn fell to the ground with a clank.

Conan parried the spear thrusts with a fierce swipe of his sword that sheared off the heads of both weapons. With a vicious thrust he impaled one antagonist on his long blade. The Turanian fell sprawling against the other with a gurgle. The second man's sword stroke at the Cimmerian's head went awry and struck sparks from the flagstones. In the next instant, the man was pincushioned with arrows. With a groan and a clatter of mail he fell.

Roused to a vicious lust for killing, Conan sprang forward and tried the copper door. Time was short. In answer to the ringing note of the horn, people thrust their heads out of casements around the square. Archers appeared on some of the roofs; he must get into the tower before the foe had time to organize a defense.

The door opened before his thrusting shoulder. Leaving ten of his men to guard against attack from the rear, Conan led the rest inside.

With a clink of mail and a flash of sword blades, ten soldiers in the white turbans of the Imperial Guard rushed against him out of a doorway. The Cimmerian's battle cry rang high as he and his followers closed with their enemies. Many a curved knife or shortened spear found its mark in Turanian vitals, but the flashing scimitars also took a heavy toll. However, the bloodiest havoc wreaked was that of Conan's cross-hilted sword. He leaped, cut, and thrust with a tigerish frenzy and speed that blurred the sight of his adversaries. In a couple of minutes, the ten Turanians lay in pools of blood, though eight silent figures in bloodstained khalats bore witness to the ferocity of the defense.

Conan swept up to the second floor, taking four steps at a stride. On this floor, he knew, the quarters of the governor were located. Pausing, he flung swift orders at his followers.

"Ten of you, search for the keys to the dungeon and free Yin Allal. The rest, take all the plunder you can carry. I'll pay the governor a visit."

As the Zuagirs, howling and laughing, stormed up and down the stairs, Conan broke the sandalwood door before him into splinters with a mighty kick. He found himself in the anteroom of the governor's apartments. Crossing the floor swiftly on sound-deadening mats, he halted in midstep. From the other side of the door before him he heard a woman's voice raised in angry expostulation.

Conan's brows drew together in a vast frown. He picked up a heavy table and heaved it against the new obstacle. With a crashing impact, the ungainly missile burst open the shattered door. He tossed the remains of the table aside and strode through.

At a table in the middle of the lamplit room stood a tall, powerful man of middle age. Conan knew him by description as Veziz Shah. Silken divans and tables laden with delicacies stood about on the rug-covered floor. On one table rested a flagon of wine with two filled goblets.

A woman rested on the divan. Her wide dark eyes held no trace of fear as she looked upon the invading barbarian. Conan gave a start. This was the girl who had accosted him in Khanyria and almost led him to his death!

No time now to mull over such matters. With a curse, the governor unsheathed his jeweled scrimitar and advanced catlike upon the Cimmerian.

"You dare invade my chambers, you red-handed rogue!" he snarled. "I have heard you are on the rove again, and I hoped for the pleasure of having your limbs torn off by wild horses. But as it is—"

He whipped forward in a swift arching stroke. Most

76

men would have been so distracted by his words as to have their throats slit by that whistling edge, but the pantherish speed of barbarian muscles saved Conan. Parrying with his hilt, he lashed out in a vicious countercut. In the exchange of blows and thrusts, he soon found he faced one of the most skilled swordsmen he had ever met.

But no civilized fencer could match the skill and speed of Conan, hardened in wars and battles since boyhood against foes from all over the world. The skill at arms he had won as a mercenary would by itself have made him master of any ordinary swordsman, for his learning had been pounded into his brain in endless, bloody strife on far battlefields. In addition he retained the flashing, lightning-quick speed of the primordial barbarian, unslowed by civilized comfort.

As the duel continued, Veziz Shah began to tire and his eyes filled with an awful fear. With a sudden cry he flung his scimitar into Conan's face and raced for the far wall. There his questing fingers probed the surface as if seeking the spring to open a hidden exit.

Conan avoided the missle with a jerk of his black-maned head. The next second his arm was around the neck and his knee in the back of the Turanian amir. His voice was a terrible whisper in Veziz Shah's ear.

"Dog, remember when you caught ten of my Af-ghulis when you commanded a squadron in Se-cunderam? And how you sent me their pickled heads in jars with wishes for a hearty repast? Your time has come. Rot in Hell!"

With a terrible heave, the blood-mad Cimmerian forced his enemy's body backwards against the thrust of his knee until the Turanian's spine snapped like a dry twig. A lifeless corpse flopped to the floor. Sweating and panting, Conan turned to the woman on the divan.

Thanara had not moved during the fight. Now she rose, eyes shining, raised her arms and came fearlessly towards Conan, ignoring the bloody sword in his hand. The blood ran swiftly through his veins at the sight of her.

"You are a real man!" she whispered, pressing herself against his rough mail and twining her arms around his corded neck. "None other could have slain Veziz Shah. I am glad you did. He forced me by threats to come in here to do his bidding."

Conan felt the hot urge of his racing blood. In his younger days he would have swept the woman into his arms and damned the consequences. But now the caution of long experience asserted itself. He growled warningly.

"You were clad otherwise when we met in Khanyria," he said, taking both her wrists in one big paw and drawing her firmly down to the couch beside him. "Tell me the tale behind that ambush, and your part in it. No lies, now, if you know what's good for you!"

The dark eyes under the long lashes regarded him without fear. A well-formed hand gently drew itself from his grasp and took one of the goblets of wine from the table. She handed him this vessel and began sipping the other herself. The assurance of a beautiful and intelligent woman colored her actions.

"You must be thirsty after killing. Have a draught of this wine. It is the best from Veziz Shah's own cellar. Drink, and I will tell you the story you ask for."

Conan stared into the depths of the cup as Thanara's musical voice began: "I am Thanara, a *yedka* or high-born lady of Maypur. King Yezdigerd has graciously appointed me one of his personal

78

agents—the eyes and ears of the king, as we call them in Turan. When word came that you had embarked on your lonely journey, I was sent to supervise the work of the stupid mercenaries engaged by our agent in Tarantia. I suppose—"

Conan hurled his cup to the floor and furiously turned upon the woman. He had sniffed the wine and let a little touch his tongue, and his keen barbarian senses told him of the threat that lurked in the cup. One huge hand fastened itself in her long black hair.

"I'll supervise you, strumpet!" he snarled. "I thought—"

Thanara's hand came up from behind her and flung into his face a pinch of the pollen of the yellow lotus. Conan jerked back, coughing and sneezing, and let go Thanara's hair. Holding her breath, she slipped out of his reach and stood up.

Snoring heavily, Conan sprawled upon the couch.

Thanara nodded in satisfaction. For the next two or three days he would be like a man stone dead. Swift action was now necessary.

A rising murmur from without attracted her attention. She stepped to a window overlooking the square and pulled back the curtains. At the sight she saw she jerked back. Houses flamed, fired by the ravaging Zuagir horde. Shrieks of captive women and curses of battling men echoed. White, ghostly shapes flitted here and there. No soldiery was to be seen. Evidently Conan had entered the fort, not alone as she had thought, but in the company of the desert wolves.

Swiftly she collected her wits. A seasoned spy, she was already hatching a plan to save herself and further the king's aims. She grabbed a white robe from one of the chests and donned it. She armed herself with a long, gold-hilted dagger. Thrusting aside the broken and staring corpse of the late governor, she searched with swift hands for the spring activating the secret door.

With a grating sound, a section of the wall swung inward, disclosing a spiral staircase leading downwards. She went back to the couch where the unconscious form of Conan rested. Grasping him beneath the armpits, she dragged him inside the secret door, straining her muscles to the utmost to move his great weight. She worked the spring from inside to close the door and laid the Cimmerian to rest on the steps. He lay snoring like a hibernating bear.

Thanara hurried down the steps. Light came faintly from several narrow window slits. On the ground floor she found herself in a small circular chamber. The exit worked in the same way as the entrance to the hidden passage. She pressed the stud and slipped out, taking good note of the means of reëntry.

The fort was a hell. The Zuagirs had broken out the contents of the wine cellars and gotten swiftly drunk, with the light-hearted irresponsibility of the primitive nomad unused to civilized drink. Their laughing torchmen had set fire to every house. Bands of captive, half-naked women were rounded up and herded, with whiplashes and coarse jests, toward the main gate.

At the barracks the slaughter had been awful. The cornered soldiers, rushing out through the only exit, had run into a hail of arrows from the waiting Zuagir archers. None of them had a chance, blinded by smoke and confused by sleep. Hundreds of pincushioned bodies lay in heaps about the ruins of the barracks, while charred bodies in the debris showed that many had been caught by the flames before they could win out the door to face the arrows.

Among the inner buildings of the fort, bands of blood-mad nomads were still cutting down the remnants of the company of the Imperial Guard who, awakened by the noise, burst out of their scattered lodgings. Such a bloody stroke as tonight's sack had not been dealt a Turanian stronghold in decades.

Hardened to a life of raw experience, Thanara hurried through the dark streets. The way was lit only by the guttering flames of burning houses. Unfrightened by the corpses choking the gutters, she melted into dark doorways whenever a screaming Zuagir band shuffled by, swinging golden spoils and herding captive women. When passing the mouth of a small lane, she heard a gurgle. She peered swiftly into the gloom and discerned a prostrate figure. She also saw that it wore the spired helmet and fine-meshed mail coif of a Turanian Imperial Guard.

Hurrying into the narrow space, she bent and removed the gag from the man's mouth. She at once recognized Ardashir of Akif, half suffocated by the smoke of nearby fires but otherwise very much alive.

She cut his bonds and motioned him to rise and follow her, stifling the imprecations that he started to gasp out by a finger at her lips. With the habits of an old soldier, he accepted her leadership without argument.

The journey back to the governor's palace was uneventful. The drunken bands seemed satisfied with their spoils and were drawing back out of the fort. Once, however, the Turanians were confronted by a pair of leering, drunken desert raiders, but the Zuagirs could not match the swift strokes of Ardashir's scimitar by clumsy motions with their curved knives. Leaving their bloodied bodies behind, the couple won unscathed to the tower. They slipped into the secret entrance. Ardashir followed unwillingly as Thanara led the way up the stairs to where Conan lay.

Recognizing his foe, Ardashir snatched at his scimitar with an oath. Thanara caught his arm. "Calm yourself! Know you not that the king will shower us with gold if we bring the barbarian to him alive?"

Ardashir made a pungent suggestion as to what King Yezdigerd could do with his gold. "The swine has smirched my honor!" he shouted. "I will—"

"Hold your tongue, fool! What will happen to you when the king learns you have lost a whole company of his precious Imperials but escaped without a scratch yourself?"

"Hm," said Ardashir, his fury abating and giving way to calculation. Thanara continued:

"The king's most skilled executioners will have to meet in conclave to invent sufferings hellish enough to atone for the trouble he has given Turan. Take hold of your senses! Will you forsake wealth and a generalship for a moment of personal vengeance?"

Growling but quieted, Ardashir sheathed his sword and helped the girl to tie the barbarian's hands and feet. Peering into the deserted quarters of the governor through a secret spyhole, she whispered:

"We shall wait until dawn. By then the Zuagir bands will have left, and we shall take horses from some stable. The drunken raiders must have overlooked some. If we spur hard, we can be out of danger in half a day. Provisions can be found in this house. We shall ride straight for the capital and drug our prisoner anew during the journey to keep him quiet. In five days he shall lie in the king's deepest dungeon in Aghrapur!"

Her dark eyes flashed triumphantly as she gazed on the prostrate form of the Cimmerian.

4. The Palace on the Cliff

WITH HEAD WHIRLING, stomach knotted with nausea, and throat parched, Conan the Cimmerian slowly regained his senses. His last memory was of sitting on the sumptuous couch of Veziz Shah, governor of Fort Wakla. Now he found himself gazing at dank, dripping walls, with the squeak of scuttling rats in his ears as he turned heavily over to sit up on a bed of moldy straw. As he moved, there was a jingle of chains linking the fetters on his wrists and ankles with a massive stone staple set in the wall. He was naked but for a loincloth.

His head felt as it it were going to split. His tongue stuck to his palate with thirst, and intense pangs of hunger assailed him. In spite of the shooting pains in his skull, he raised his voice in a mighty bellow.

"Ho, guards! Would you let a man perish of hunger and thirst? Fetch food and drink! What cursed nook of Hell is this?"

With a patter cf footsteps and a jingle of keys, a paunchy, bearded jailer appeared on the other side of the iron grille that barred the door of the cell. "So the western dog has awakened! Know that these are the dungeons of King Yezdigerd's palace at Aghrapur. Here are food and water. You will need to fill your belly to appreciate the cordial reception the king has prepared for you."

Thrusting a loaf and a small jug through the bars,

the jailer went away, his cackling laughter resounding hollowly in the corridor. The famished Cimmerian flung himself on the food and drink. He munched great hunks of the stale loaf and washed them down with gulps of water. At least he did not now have to fear poison, for if the king had wanted to kill him out of hand it would have been easy to do so while he lay unconscious.

He pondered his predicament. He was in the hands of his most implacable enemy. In the olden days King Yezdigerd had offered fabulous rewards for Conan's head. Many had been the attempts on Conan. Several would-be assassins had been killed by Conan himself. But the tenacious hatred in Yezdigerd's heart had not slackened even when his foe had won power as king of far Aquilania. Now, by a woman's devious schemes, Conan was at last at the mercy of his merciless antagonist. Any ordinary man would have been daunted by the terrible prospect.

Not so Conan! Accepting things as they were with barbarian stolidity, his fertile mind was already trying and discarding plans of winning to freedom and turning the tables of his vengeful captor. His eyes narrowed as the clank of footsteps sounded in the corridor.

At a harsh word of command the steps halted. Through the grille Conan could discern a half-score of guardsmen, gilt-worked mail a-shimmer in the torchlight, curved swords in their hands. Two bore heavy bows at the ready. A tall, massive officer stood forward. Conan recognized Ardashir, who spoke in a sharp, cutting voice.

"Shapur and Vardan! Truss the barbarian securely and sling a noose about his neck! Archers! Stand by to prevent any trick!"

The two soldiers stepped forward to carry out the

order. One bore a log of wood six feet long and several inches thick, while the other carried a stout rope. Ardashir addressed himself to the Cimmerian. His eyes glowed with malevolence and his fingers twitched with eagerness to attack Conan, but he held himself in check with the iron self-control of a well-trained officer. He hissed: "One false move, barbarian dog, and your heart shall know the marksmanship of my archers! I should dearly love to slay you myself, but you are the king's own meat."

Conan's chill blue eyes regarded the maddened officer without emotion as the soldiers placed the log across his shoulders and bound his arms to it. Without apparent effort, Conan tensed his huge arm muscles, so that the rope was stretched to its greatest tautness at the moment of tying. The jailer than unlocked Conan's fetters. Conan rumbled:

"You Turanian dogs will get what you deserve sooner or later. You will see."

Ardashir's face twitched in fury as he spat back: "And you will get yours, you red-handed rogue! No torture devised by human brains will be too cruel when the royal executioners set to work upon you." He laughed a shrill uncontrolled laugh that betrayed his hysteric mood. "But enough of this gabble. Follow me, Your Majesty of maggoty Aquilonia!"

At a gesture to the guardsmen, the little company marched along the dank corridors. The bound barbarian walked in their midst, bearing the log across his shoulders. Conan was quite unruffled. He had been in many tight places before and won his way to freedom. He was like a trapped wolf, alert and constantly looking for a chance to reverse the situation. He did not waste thought on the terrible odds against him, or on futile recriminations against his foes, or on self-reproach for the moment's lapse in vigilance that resulted in his capture. His whole mind and nervous system were concentrated on what to do next.

Winding stone staircases led upward. As nobody had blindfolded Conan, his keen eyes took in every detail. The dungeons of the royal palace were far below ground level. There were several floors to pass, at each of which an armed guard stood ready with sword or pike.

Twice Conan glimpsed the outside world as they passed window slits. The darkling sky showed that the time was either dawn or dusk. Now he understood the mystifying murmur of surf which had reached his ears. The palace was built on the outskirts of Aghrapur, on a crag overlooking the Sea of Vilayet. The dungeons were carved out of the heart of the rock whose sheer face ended in the lapping waves below. That was why Conan could see the sky through the window slits, though they had not yet reached the lower floors of the palace itself. Conan stored the knowledge in his mind.

The size of the palace was amazing. The party passed through endless rooms with fountains and jeweled vases. Exotic blooms exuded heavy perfumes. Now their steps echoed from arching walls; now they were muffled by rich rugs and hangings. Corseleted soldiers stood like statues everywhere with inscrutable faces and eyes alert. Here the splendor of the East bloomed in its full glory.

The party halted before two gigantic, gold-worked doors. Fully fifty feet high they towered, their upper parts disappearing in the gloom. Mysterious arabesques curled their snaky course across the surfaces of the doors, on which the dragons, heroes, and wizards of Hyrkanian legend were depicted. Ardashir stepped forward and struck the golden plates a ringing blow with the hilt of his scrimitar.

In response, the immense doors opened slowly. The low murmur of a great assembly of people reached Conan's ears.

The throne room was vaster than anything Conan had ever seen, from the sumptuous state chambers of Ophir and Nemedia to the smoky, timber-roofed halls of Asgard and Vanaheim. Giant pillars of marble reared lofty columns toward a roof that seemed as distant as the sky. The profusion of cressets, lamps, and candelabra illuminated costly drapes, paintings, and hangings. Behind the throne rose windows of stained glass, closed against the fall of night.

A glittering host filled the hall. Fully a thousand must have assembled there. There were Nemedians in jupons, trunk hose, and leathern boots; Ophireans in billowing cloaks; stocky, black-bearded Shemites in silken robes; renegade Zuagirs from the desert; Vendhyans in bulging turbans and gauzy robes; barbarically-clad emissaries from the black kingdoms to the far southwest. Even a lone yellow-haired warrior from the Far North, clad in a somber black tunic, stared sullenly before him, his powerful hands gripping the hilt of a heavy longsword that rested before him with the chape of its scabbard on the floor.

Some had come here to escape the wrath of their own rulers, some as informers and traitors against the lands of their birth, and some as envoys. The gluttonous mind of King Yezdigerd was never satisfied with the size of his growing empire. Many and devious were the ways in which he sought to enlarge it.

The blare of golden trumpets rang across the huge hall. An avenue opened through the milling mass, and Conan's little group set itself again in motion. The distance to the dais was still too great to make out the individuals clustered there, but their brisk approach would soon bring them into range.

Conan was afire with curiosity. Though he had fought this eastern despot many years ago on several occasions—as war-chief of the Zuagirs, as admiral of the Vilayet pirates, as leader of the Himelian hillmen, and as hetman of the *kozaki*—he had never yet seen his implacable foe in person. He kept his eyes full on the figure on the golden throne as he approached it.

So it came about that he did not notice the widening of the blond giant's gray eyes in sudden recognition. The powerful knuckles whitened as the enigmatic gaze intently followed the towering figure of the Cimmerian on his way toward the dais.

King Yezdigerd was a swarthy giant of a man with a short black beard and a thin, cruel mouth. Although the debauchery of the Turanian court had wrought pouches under his glittering eyes, and lines crisscrossed his stern and gloomy features ten years too early, his hard-muscled, powerful body bore witness that self-indulgence had not sapped his immense vitality.

A brilliant strategist and an insatiable plunderer, Yezdigerd had more than doubled the size of the kingdom inherited from his weak predecessor Yildiz. He had wrung tribute from the city-states of Brythunia and eastern Shem. His gleaming horsemen had beaten the armies of such distant nations as Stygia and Hyperborea. The crafty king of Zamora, Mithridates, had been shorn of border provinces and had kept his throne only at the price of groveling before his conqueror.

Arrayed in a splendor of silk and cloth-of-gold, the king lolled on the shining throne with the deceptive ease of a resting panther.

At his right sat a woman. Conan felt his blood run hot with recognition. Thanara! Her voluptuous body was draped in the seductive robes of a Turanian noblewoman. A diamond-studded diadem glittered in her lustrous black hair. Her eyes fastened triumphantly on the trussed and weaponless figure of her captive. She joined in the laughter of the courtiers round the throne at some grim jest uttered by the king.

The detail halted before the throne. Yezdigerd's eyes blazed with triumphant glee. At last he held in his power the man who had slaughtered his soldiers, burnt his cities, and scuttled his ships. The lust for vengeance churned up within him, but he held himself in check while the guardsmen knelt and touched their foreheads to the marble floor.

Conan made no obeisance. His blue eyes aflame with icy fire, he stood still and upright, clashing with the Turanian king in a battle of looks. Every inch of his body expressed defiance and contempt. Unclad as he was, he still commanded the attention of all by the aura of power that radiated from him. The rumor of his fabulous exploits was whispered back and forth among the members of the glittering throng. Many knew him under other dreaded names in their own distant lands.

Sensing the strain upon the rope he held, Ardashir looked up from his kneeling posture. Black rage seethed in his face as he saw the disdain of the Cimmerian for court etiquette. He tugged viciously at the rope, tightening the noose about Conan's neck. A lesser man would have stumbled and fallen, but Conan stood steady as a rock. The massive muscles of his bull-neck swelled in ridges against the pressure of the rope. Then he suddenly bent forward and straightened up again, pulling the rope backwards. Ardashir was jerked off his knees and sprawled with a clatter of gear on the marble.

"I pay homage to no Hyrkanian dog!" Conan's roar was like a peal of thunder. "You wage your wars with the help of women. Can you handle a sword yourself? I'll show you how a real man fights!"

During his short speech, Conan relaxed the taut muscles of his arms, so that the rope binding them went slack. By stretching, he got the tips of his left fingers around one end of the log on his back. With a quick jerk he slipped his right arm out of the loose coils of rope and brought the log around in front of him. Then he swiftly freed his left arm.

Ardashir scrambled up and lunged towards him, drawing his scimitar. Conan whipped the end of the log around with a thud against the Turanian's helmet. The officer was hurled across the floor, his body spinning like that of a thrown doll.

For a split second, everybody stood unmoving, struck still by this seemingly magical feat. With the fighting instinct of the barbarian, Conan took instant advantage of this pause. One end of the log shot out and caught a guardsman in the face. The man flew over backwards, his face a mere smear of blood and broken bones. Then Conan whirled and threw the log into the nearest group of guards on the other side of him, even as they started to rise and draw their weapons. The men were bowled over in a clattering heap.

Lithe and quick as a leopard, Conan bounded forward, snatching up the scimitar that Ardashir had dropped when knocked unconscious. A couple of courtiers tried to bar the Cimmerian's way at the foot of King Yezdigerd's dais, but he easily cut his path through them, slashing and thrusting. He bounded up the steps of the dais.

As he came, the king rose to meet him, sweeping out his own scimitar. The jewels in its hilt flashed as Yezdigerd brought the blade up to parry a terrific right cut that Conan aimed at his head. Such was the force of the blow that the king's sword snapped. Conan's blade cut through the many folds of the snow-white turban, cleaving the spray of bird-of-paradise feathers that rose from the front of it and denting the steel cap that Yezdigerd wore beneath.

Though the blow failed to split the king's skull as Conan intended, it threw the Turanian backwards, stunned. Yezdigerd fell back over the arm of his throne and overset the gleaming chair. King and throne rolled off the dais, down the steps on the other side, and into a knot of onrushing guardsmen, spoiling their charge.

Conan, beside himself with battle lust, would have bounded after the king to finish him off. But loyal arms dragged Yezdigerd out of the press, and from all sides sword blades and spear points pressed in upon the unprotected Cimmerian.

Conan's scimitar wove a lethal net of steel around him. He surpassed himself in brilliant swordsmanship. Despite his stay in the dungeon and the after-effects of the drug he had inhaled, he was fired with vitality. If he must die, he would now die sword in hand, laughing and slaying, to carve a niche for himself in the Hall of Heroes.

He whirled in gleeful frenzy. A quick slash sent an antagonist tumbling backwards with his entrails spilling out; a lightning thrust burst through mail links into a Turanian heart. Stabbing, slicing, smiting, and thrusting, he wrought red havoc. For an instant, raging like a mad elephant about the dais, he cleared it of soldiers and courtiers except for those who lay in a tangle about his feet.

Only the lady Thanara remained, sitting petrified in her chair. With a grating laugh, Conan tore the glittering diadem from her hair and flung her into the throng that milled about the platform.

Soldiers now advanced grimly from all sides, their spearheads and sword blades forming a bristling hedge in front of an ordered line of shields. Behind them, archers nocked their shafts. Noncombatants stood in clumps in the farther parts of the throne room, watching fascinated.

Conan flexed his muscles, swung his scimitar, and gave a booming laugh. Blood ran down his naked hide from superficial cuts in scalp, arm, chest, and leg. Surrounded and unarmored, not even his strength and speed could save him from the thrust of many keen blades all at once. The prospect of death did not trouble him; he only hoped to take as many foes as he could into the darkness with him.

Suddenly there came the clash of steel, the spurt of blood, and the icy gleam of a northern longsword. A giant figure hewed its way through the armored lines, leaving three blood-spattered corpses on the floor. With a mighty bound, the fair-haired northerner leaped to the dais. In his left arm he cradled a couple of heavy, round objects—bucklers of bronze and leather picked up from the floor where the victims of Conan's first outburst had dropped them.

"Catch this!" cried the newcomer, tossing one of the shields to Conan. Their glances met and locked. Conan cried:

"Rolf! What do you here, old polar bear?"

"I will tell you later," growled the northerner, grasping the handle of the other buckler. "If we live, that is. If not, I am prepared to fight and die with you."

The unexpected advent of this formidable ally raised Conan's spirits even higher.

"Rush in, jackals," he taunted, waving his blood-stained scimitar. "Who will be the next to consign his soul to Hell? Attack, damn you, or I'll carry the fight to you!"

The steel-sheathed ranks of the Turanian soldiery had halted, forming a square about the dais. The two giant barbarians stood back to back, one black-haired and almost naked, the other blond and clad in somber black. They seemed like two royal tigers surrounded by timorous hunters, none of whom dared to strike the first blow.

"Archers!" cried an officer directing the Turanian troopers. "Spread out, so the shafts shall strike from all sides."

"They have us," growled Rolf "Had we but stout coats of Asgardean mail . . . Ah, well, it was fun while it lasted."

"Not quite," said Conan. "See you that row of windows? Here is my plan . . ."

He whispered a few quick words to his comrade, who nodded. The two giants sprang forward, their blades flickering with the speed of striking snakes. Two guardsmen sank to the floor in their blood, and the others shrank back momentarily from the fury of the onslaught.

"Follow me, Rolf! We'll fool these dogs yet!" barked the Cimmerian, striking right and left.

The swords of the barbarians cleared a bloody avenue. The big northerner wheeled, thrusting and cutting, his sword cutting down the Turanians like wheat stalks before the scythe as he guarded Conan's back. As Conan rushed forward, Rolf followed in his wake, his sword widening the bloody path opened by the Cimmerian. His booming bass was casting forth the ringing tones of old northern battle songs, and the gleam of the berserk was in his gaze.

None could stand before their terrible attack. Turanian swords and spears sought their blood, but glanced harmlessly from the shields as the pantherish speed of the barbarians blurred the eyes of their adversaries. Conan bled from a score of wounds and Rolf's garb was in tatters, but the bodies heaped upon the floor bespoke the violence of their attack.

They put their backs to one of the large windows. For a few seconds both barbarians exploded into maniacal fury, laying about them with blood-crusted blades and clearing a space of several feet around them. The massed soldiers shrank back for a moment. It seemed to their superstitious minds as if these were not men but invincible ogres, hard as steel, risen from the darker realms to wreak terrible vengeance.

Conan utilized this moment with lightninglike speed. The stained glass of the window shattered into thousands of gleaming, many-colored shards under blows from his scimitar that tore a great gap in the leaded pane. Hurling their swords and shields into the faces of their foes, the Cimmerian and the northerner sprang through in headlong dives toward the sea two hundred feet below. A taunting laugh lingered behind them in the air as the guardsmen closed in.

"Archers! An archer, quickly, to have at them!" The commanding officer's voice was shrill with desperation. Five men stood forward, each armed with the powerful, double-curved Hyrkanian war bow. The window niche was cleared, and soon the twang of cords was heard. Then one of the bowmen shrugged his shoulders and turned to the officer,

"The range is too great in this treacherous moonlight. We cannot even discern their heads, and probably they are swimming under water most of the time. The task is beyond us."

Glaring, the general swung about and hurried to the king's chamber. Yezdigerd had recovered from his shock. The only sign of damage was a small bandage round his forehead, partly covered by his turban. The terse account of the incidents elapsed was interrupted by the crash of the king's fist on a table, spilling vases and wine jugs to the floor.

"You have dared to fail! The red-handed barbarians have escaped and mocked the majesty of Turan! Are my soldiers sucklings, that they cannot lay two men low? Every tenth man among the guards shall die in the morning, to bolster the courage of the rest!"

He continued in a lower voice: "See that two war galleys are outfitted at once. The barbarians will surely try to steal a boat and make their way across the sea. We shall overtake them. See that the ships are well-provisioned and manned by my best seamen and soldiers. Take the sturdiest slaves for rowers. When I have caught these dogs, they shall suffer the agonies of a thousand deaths in the torture chambers of Aghrapur!"

He laughed, animated by the grisly prospect, and gestured imperiously to his general. The latter hurried out, threading his way through the throng in the courtroom to carry out his lord's commands.

Khosru the fisherman sat patiently on the gunwale of his sloop, mending a net which had been broken by the thrashing of a giant sturgeon that afternoon. He cursed his misfortune, for this was a fine net. It had cost him two pieces of gold and the promise of fifty pounds of fish to the Shemite merchant from whom he

95

had bought it. But what could a poor, starving fisherman do? He must have nets to get his living from the sea.

Aye, if those were the only things necessary for him and his family! But he must also strain and work to meet the taxes imposed by the king. He looked up in venomous, furtive hatred at the palace, limned against the moonlit sky. It perched on the cliff like a giant vulture of gold and marble. The king's taxgatherers had supple whips and no compunction about using them. Welts and old scars on Khosru's back told of wrongs suffered when the shoals were empty of fish.

Suddenly the sloop heaved, almost unseating him. Khosru sprang up, his eyes starting from their sockets in terror. A huge, almost-naked man was climbing aboard, his black, square-cut hair disordered and dripping. He seemed to Khosru like some demon of the sea, an evil merman, come up from unknown deeps to blast his soul and devour his body.

For a moment the apparition simply sat on a thwart, breathing in deep gasps. Then it spoke in Hyrkanian, though with a barbarous accent. Khosru took heart a little, for the tales depicted the demons as devoid of speech. Still he quavered before the smoldering eyes and ferocious mien of the giant. His terror increased as another figure, a huge, black-clad, golden-haired man with a broad-bladed dagger at his belt, followed the first over the gunwale.

"Fear not, sailor!" boomed the black-haired giant. "We don't want your blood, only your ship." He drew a glittering diadem from the waistband of his loincloth and held it out. "Here is payment enough and more. You can buy ten such craft as this one with it. Agreed—or—?"

He flexed his thick fingers suggestively. Khosru, his

head whirling, nodded and snatched the diadem. With the speed of a frightened mouse he scuttled into the dinghy moored to the stern of the sloop and rowed away at desperate speed.

His strange customers lost no time. The sail went swiftly up and billowed in the freshening breeze. The trim craft gathered speed as it steered out toward the east.

Khosru shrugged his shoulders, mystified. He paused to hold up the fabulous diadem, whose gems glittered in the moonlight like a cascade of splashing white fire.

5.   The Sea of Blood

THE WIND blew hard. Salt spray was tossed from the waves by the howling gusts. Conan the Cimmerian expanded his mighty chest in deep, joyous breaths, relishing the feel of freedom. Many memories crowded his mind from the earlier days when he, as chief of the pirates of Vilayet, had swept the sea with dripping sword blades and laid the Turanian seaports in smoking ruins.

Vilayet was still a Hyrkanian sea, dominated by the Turanian navy's swift war galleys. Trade was carried on to some extent by daring merchants from the smaller countries on the northeastern shore, but a merchantman's way across the turbulent waves was fraught with peril. No state of war was needed for a Turanian captain to board, plunder, and scuttle a foreign vessel if it pleased him. The excuse was simply "infringement upon the interests of the lord of the Turanian Empire."

Besides the greedy Turanian navy, there lurked another danger as great: the pirates!

A motley horde of escaped slaves, criminals, freebooters, and wandering adventurers, all with a common lust for gold and a common disregard for human life, infested the waters of this huge inland sea, making even Turanian shipping a hazardous venture. In the mazes of islands to the south and east lay their secret harbors.

Internal strife often crippled their power, to the satisfaction of the king of Turan, until there came among them a strange barbarian from the West, with blue eyes and raven hair. Conan swept aside their quarreling captains and took the reins of leadership in his own hands. He united the pirates and forged them into a fearsome weapon aimed at the heart of Turan. Conan smiled in recollection of those days, when his name was a curse in Vilayet harbors, and prayers and incantations were chanted against him in the temples of the seaports.

The sloop was a trim and well-built craft. Her sharp bow cut the water like a scimitar, and her single sail billowed tautly before the wind. Aghrapur had been astern for nearly twenty hours. Conan guessed their speed to be greater than that of Turanian warships. Should the breeze die, however, they would have a problem. They could never hope to equal the speed of a galley, propelled by hard-driven slave rowers, by means of their own puny sweeps. But the wind showed no sign of slackening, and Rolf's capable hand guided the small vessel before it so as to extract the last ounce of sailpower from it.

Rolf was telling the long tale of the wanderings and adventures that had led him to Aghrapur. ". . . so here I am, a fugitive from my native Asgard and from Turan both."

"Why did you join me?" asked Conan. "You were comfortably off at the Turanian court."

Rolf looked offended. "Did you think I had forgotten the time you saved my life, in that battle with the Hyperboreans in the Graaskal Mountains?"

Conan grinned. "So I did, didn't I? After so many battles, I had forgotten myself." He shaded his eyes and looked at the unbroken blue line of the horizon. "I doubt not that at least a couple of Yezdigerd's war galleys are on our heels," he said grimly. "The rascal must be hot for vengeance. I doubt he will soon forget how we pulled his beard."

"True," rumbled Rolf. "I hope this fine wind keeps up, or we shall soon be at grips with his galleys."

Conan's active mind was already dwelling on another topic. "In my days with the Red Brotherhood," he mused, "this area was the surest one for a sweep to catch a fat merchantman from Sultanapur or Khawarizm. Aye, but those traders fought well; sometimes the sea was red with our blood as well as theirs before we had the prize. Some of the pirate ships should be nearby." His eagle eyes continued to scan the endless blue vista.

He stiffened like a lion sighting its prey and thrust out an arm to starboard.

"Rolf, we have company! Those yellow sails can mean but one thing: a pirate. We might as well drop our sail and await them; they could overtake us in a half-hour if they wished!"

Eyes fixed on the oncoming vessel, he waited, outwardly stolid and unmoved.

Conan drank in the measured thump of oars in their locks, the creak of spars, the shouts of boatswains, and the smell of tar with gusto. Half a cable's length away a slim sailing galley, its yellow sail ablaze in the afternoon sun, hove to. The black flag of the Brotherhood fluttered from its masthead. Conan and Rolf rowed toward the pirate craft.

The gunwale was lined with faces. Many were swathed in colorful headcloths. Some favored the eastern turban; others wore helmets of steel or bronze. A few had pates shaven and bare except for a scalplock. The din and clamor lessened. Cold, cruel eyes scrutinized the two strangers in the sloop.

The small craft bumped against the side of the big-ger vessel. A rope was lowered. Hand over hand, Conan and Rolf climbed with the agility of prac-ticed seamen. Clearing the gunwale, they found themselves in the center of a half-circle of curious pi-rates, all shouting queries at once. Among them Co-nan recognized several who had followed him in former days. He snarled:

"Dogs, don't you know me? Is your memory so short that you must be reminded of my name, or have your eyes grown dim with age?"

Several men in the throng had drawn back, blanching from the shock of recognition. One, white-faced, rasped:

"A ghost, by Tarim! Erlik preserve us! It is our old admiral, come back from his grave to haunt us!" Veteran though he was, the grizzled pirate was ob-viously terrified as he pointed at Conan. "You per-ished many years ago, when the vampires of the Colchian Mountains assailed your crew as they fled from the Turanians after taking vengeance on Ar-taban of Shahpur. Begone, spirit, or we shall all be doomed!"

Conan gave a gusty laugh. He slapped his thigh with mirth, plucked Rolf's dagger from its sheath, and hurled it to the deck so that the point was driven inches deep into the planking and the hilt quivered upright. Then he pulled the weapon out.

"Have you taken leave of your senses, Artus?" he roared. "Could a ghost make that nick in the deck? Come, man, I am as alive as the lot of you and, if you believe me not, I'll crack a few heads to prove it! I escaped both the vampires and the Turanians, and what befell me after that is no concern of yours. Do you know me now?"

Conan's old followers now joyfully milled about the

towering Cimmerian to shake his hand and clap his back. Men who had never seen him before crowded with the others, fired with curiosity about a man whose name was legendary, and whose fantastic exploits were still told by the wine legs on still evenings.

Suddenly a sharp voice sheared through the clamor: "Avast, there! What's going on? Who are they? I told you to fetch them to me as soon as they were picked up!"

A tall man, wearing a light mail shirt, stood on the bridge, one fist banging the rails. A blazing red cloth was wound around his head. A badly-healed scar from eye to chin disfigured his long, narrow face.

"It is Conan, Captain!" cried old Artus, the shipmaster. "Our old admiral has returned!"

The captain's close-set eyes narrowed as his own sight sought confirmation of the oldster's words. An evil light blazed in those eyes as he picked out the bronzed form of the Cimmerian. He opened his mouth to speak, but Conan beat him to it.

"Are you not glad to see me, Yanak? Remember how I kicked you out of the fleet for hoarding spoils that belonged to all? How have you managed to trick your way to a captaincy? Ill days must have dawned for the Brotherhood!"

With his mouth working, Yanak spat back: "For that, barbarian, I will have you hung by the heels and roasted over the ship's fire! I am captain and give the orders here!"

"That may be," retorted Conan. "But I am still a member of the Brotherhood." He looked challengingly around, and nobody chose to deny his assertion. "I claim a right according to the articles. The right of any member of the brotherhood to fight the captain of a ship for the captaincy in a captain's duel."

102

He tossed up the dagger he had borrowed from Rolf and caught it again. It was a formidable weapon with a broad, eighteen-inch blade, but still no sword. He and Rolf had cast aside their swords in order to swim to the sloop, so the dagger was the only weapon they had between them.

The crew murmured, for all knew that in such a duel Conan would have to fight with whatever weapon he had with him at the time, while Yanak could choose what weapons he pleased. Yanak's armor, too, would give him a further advantage.

"This is madness, Conan!" Artus plucked the Cimmerian's elbow. "Yanak will cut you to pieces. I have seen him fight three brawling drunkards at the time and lay them low. We'll depose him instead and choose you for captain. All your old followers are on your side."

Conan shook his head and rumbled: "Half the crew don't know me and would oppose such a move. The men would be split into factions and our strength would be weakened. No, it must be done the traditional way."

Several crewmen were already clearing a space around the mast. Yanak approached, a gleeful smile on his scarred face as his hands tested the supple strength of a keen, straight sword. It was a weapon forged by a master craftsman, as could be seen by its brightly gleaming blade and sharply honed edges, tapering to a needle point.

Conan gripped his dagger firmly and strode towards the mast. A wide circle six yards in diameter was already drawn in charcoal on the deck around the mast. The rules of the fight were simple. The antagonists were to fight inside the circle. Any trick was allowed. The fight would be to the death, or until one of the duellists was so badly hurt he could not go on. In that case he would simply be flung over-board anyway. If one of the fighters stepped out of the circle, the onlookers would at once thrust him back in.

The instant Conan entered the circle, Yanak bounded forward, cleaving the air with a whistling stroke. But the barbarian was too old a hand to be surprised. He leaped sideways, and Yanak was saved from a dagger thrust in his side only by twisting his body aside at the last moment. After that, he moved more warily, although he was clearly at an advantage. The longer reach of his weapon almost matched him evenly with Conan's brawn and stature. Now and then he made a sudden attack, shouting and cursing, but the silent Cimmerian parried or evaded the blows with effortless ease and continued to circle around the mast. Conan ignored the pirate captain's taunts and exhortations to stand and fight.

Then Yanak tried a trick. Conan and he were temporarily on the same side of the mast. With all the power of his knotted leg muscles, the captain sprang upward in a mighty leap, at the same time smiting downward at the Cimmerian's bare head.

But Conan's instinct triggered his lightning-fast responses. Instead of retreating, he sprang forward. Yanak's blade whistled harmlessly down behind the barbarian's back as Conan buried his knife to the hilt in his foe's abdomen, shearing through the light mail links with the immense force of his thrust. The pirate fell to the deck, cursing and gagging on blood. His sword fell with a clank. Conan stooped and lifted him up. With a mighty heave, he flung the corpse over the heads of the crew into the sea. Picking up the fallen sword, he swept their ranks with a cold gaze.

"Now who is captain, my lads?"

The shouts of "Conan!" would have satisfied any

doubter. Conan drank in the heady staisfaction of his new-won power. Then his thunderous voice bellowed them to silence.

"To the sails and oars, lubbers! A man to the masthead as lookout! I have Yezdigerd himself hot on my trail. But we will lead him a merry chase, by Crom!"

Taken aback by the announcement that their archenemy was abroad, the crew's idolatrous confidence in Conan was yet so strong as to wash away all misgivings. Many remembered how the Cimmerian had fought and tricked his way out of seemingly impossible odds. Tales of these exploits were circulated among the rest of the crew.

Conan sprang to the bridge in one mighty leap, shouting: "Set sail! Course southeast!"

Men hauled at lines, voicing lusty sea songs. Yellow canvas spread before the breeze. The pirate at the helm strained with knotted muscles at the steering oar, bringing the slim vessel about. She fled eastward before the wind, fleet as the deer of the moorlands.

"So you think I'm mad, Artus? By Crom, I hope Yezdigerd thinks so too!"

Conan's hearty laughter resounded in the well-appointed cabin as he sprawled in a chair, a tumbler of wine in his hand. Conan had casually possessed himself of the wardrobe of his predecessor and clad himself in the colorful garb of a Vilayet pirate: scarlet breeches, flaring sea boots, a yellow shirt of fine Vendhyan silk with wide sleeves, and a wide, varicolored sash around his waist. The costume was topped off by a red cloth around his head. Into the sash was thrust a long dirk with an ornately-carved ivory handle.

Together with Rolf, Artus the shipmaster lounged

in Conan's company while the galley swiftly cleaved the waters of the inland sea. With clouded brow, he set his goblet on the table.

"No, Conan, I know you too well. But this seems a hare-brained scheme, dashing straight into the jaws of the Turanian. You could at least tell us what you are planning. The men are drunk with confidence and do not think of the fact that Yezdigerd will bring at least two large war galleys. I am old and sober enough to stop and ponder. What are your intentions?"

With sudden gravity, Conan rose and went to a gilded wooden cupboard. Opening it, he brought out a roll of parchment. This he spread upon the table. It was a chart of the waters they were now sailing.

"Here is our position. Yezdigerd has been four days on his way from Aghrapur. The Turanian ships are running free. With their mean speed, I compute them to be somewhere in this area." (He pointed to a spot on the chart.) "With our present course and speed, we shall rendezvous with Yezdigerd somewhere off the Zhurazi Archipelago."

"The Zhurazi, eh?" muttered Artus. "Those are dangerous waters. The charts show no soundings. That cursed cluster is shunned by sane men. Some say it is haunted by demons and monsters from the darker realms and that you are lost if you set foot on its shores."

"Lost, Hell!" rumbled Conan. "I once lived on the north main island for a fortnight after shipwreck. There was a tribe of yellow savages dwelling among the crags, and I had the devil of a time stopping them from sacrificing me to their lizard-god!"

Thus lightly he dismissed the hair-raising drama played out on these islands years before. The pantherish Cimmerian had not only stayed alive in a land of hostile people but also had slain the monster out of forgotten ages that terrorized the inhabitants. Conan was not wont to dwell upon the past; the violent and colorful present held all his attention.

He stood for a while in silence, regarding the chart. Then, with a sudden gesture, he swept it off the table and swung about to face his friends.

"Right you are, Artus. There are no soundings on this chart. Turanian, isn't it? Drawn by the king's own surveyors in Aghrapur—the very type of map our bloodthirsty pursuer will have. That is our advantage."

And however they pressed him, he would not explain further.

Muscles played on the sweating backs of the slaves at the oars. The blades rose and fell in steady rhythm, speeding the huge war vessel over the waves. The burly slavemaster strode the catwalk with his braided whip, his skin gleaming with sweat and oil. Now and then the whiplash uncurled like a striking cobra, to hiss out and mark the back of a faltering oarsman. The slaves of Turanian ships were cruelly driven, and none so cruelly as those in King Yezdigerd's own flagship, the *Scimitar*.

The king took his ease on a silken couch on the poop, shaded by an awning and sipping wine from a golden beaker. On a similar bed by his side lounged the lady Thanara.

The king was sunk in one of his spells of gloom. His gaze was brooding and somber, as he slowly swirled the pale-yellow liquid in the golden bowl. He said:

"Evil powers aid the Cimmerian devil! He must have stolen a boat immediately upon his escape. My cursed admirals need half a day to put my flagship to sea, and then the devils that ruin human patience have turned the wind against us. We move like snails."

"Better than he can do, though," said Thanara, looking lazily at the monarch from under long eyelashes. "His puny oars will avail him little in this wind. Every stroke of the club on the block lessens his head start. Be patient, my lord! Erlik will deliver the barbarian into our hands."

"My henchmen have often thought so, yet that scoundrel has tricked his way out of every trap. Now for once I am the hunter! I will personally see that he escapes not. By the beard of my father Yildiz, there will be a reckoning!" Yezdigerd's voice became eager and his eyes filled with new energy. He shaded his face and looked out over the glittering waters.

He made a quick gesture. The admiral hurried forward, the gilded scales of his mail winking in the sunlight.

"I see land, Uthghiz. Have we veered from our course?" said the king.

The admiral, knowing his sovereign's irascible temper, quickly unfolded a map and pointed.

"That, my lord, is the Zhurazi Archipelago. The Cimmerian has probably landed there for food and water. I intend to scan the coast for signs of his boat. Furthermore, the straightest course for the eastern shores of Vilayet leads close to these islands."

"You may be right. But keep every man alert. How close can you sail?"

"These are unknown waters, my lord. The conditions of life on the islands are shrouded in superstition. Horrible tales are told of fiendish monsters haunting the crags. No surveying has been done in this area. We dare not go too close lest we strike unseeen rocks." but the *yedka* continued to scan the ragged coastline.

The king sank back on his gilded couch, muttering,

Had her eyes deceived her? Was that a sail she glimpsed before it disappeared behind a rocky islet on the fringe of the cluster? The Turanian ships drew closer with every oar stroke. She waited eagerly for another glimpse of the sail.

She stiffened and pointed. The sail had reappeared.

"Look, my lord!" she cried. "Yonder is a prize for your ships! A pirate! We have surprised them!"

The *yedka* was not the only one who spied the corsair. Swift orders were shouted. The crew prepared for battle, while signals were run up to warn the sister vessel to do likewise.

The overseers moved among the benches to check the fetters chaining the rowers. Stacks of arms were readied by the mast, and the ship's soldiery ran to their stations. Archers climbed into the rigging to suitable points of vantage, while groups of burly seamen, armed with grapnels, stood by the gunwales.

Though Conan's sharp eyes could not discern the details of these preparations, he knew that they began as soon as he let his ship be sighted. The pirate ship was long since ready for battle. Despite the heavy odds against the pirate crew, all trusted their barbaric captain implicitly. Men who had sailed with Conan years ago told fantastic tales about former sea fights and the ingenious ways the Cimmerian had turned the tables on his foes. Keen blades were shaken at the distant Turanian ships, while bearded mouths muttered oaths in many tongues.

"Prepare to go about." The sharp voice of their captain cut like steel through the din.

The order was a shock to the crew. Here they were, ready for the attack, with the greatest captain in the world to lead them—and what did this captain do? Prepare to run like a rabbit! Bewildered, they went halfheartedly to their chores. Conan noticed their listlessness and snarled:

"Be swift, you mangy rascals, or I'll have your backs raw under the lash! Do you think I'm fool enough to fight two war galleys, each with twice my strength, on the open sea, when I have a better plan? Do not worry, lubbers, we shall have a feasting of swords that songs will be written about. Now go to it!"

Fired with new enthusiasm, the men sprang into the rigging. Soon the ship was speeding toward the inner parts of the Zhurazi Archipelago. Before putting his plan into operation, Conan conferred with the ship's carpenter. The information gleaned, together with his own knowledge of the waters, left him no doubts.

The Zhurazi Archipelago was made up of two large islands surrounded by a great number of smaller isles. The strait between the two main islands was a long, narrow channel, and for this Conan guided his ship. There was grim expectation in his mien as he viewed the Turanian galleys following astern, their oars laboring with all the power that could be wrung from the slaves.

King Yezdigerd paced the poop, armed in silvered Turanian mail and a gold-spired helmet. He bore a round, emblazoned shield on his left arm; a long scimitar hung by his side. The cruel and gloomy Turanian monarch was also a fierce and intrepid warrior, who loved to take part in a good fight in person.

"See how the yellow hyenas flee!" he cried. "Will they play games with us? They will lose the wind among the islands, and then our oars will make them easy prey. Faster!"

Meanwhile the admiral conferred in low tones with the shipmaster, who argued his point with many gestures and headshakings. The admiral, looking doubtful, went back up to the poop. He said:

"Your Majesty, these waters are unsounded. We have no charts we can trust, and the shipmaster fears we shall ground. I suggest we circle the islands and catch the corsair in open sea."

Yezdigerd's voice swept aside the misgivings of his admiral with a sweeping gesture. His voice was hot with exasperation.

"I told you the rascal will be an easy prey in the lee of the islands. Let the whips be plied to bring us every ounce of speed. We shall snap our jaws about the pirate soon enough!"

The king seemed to have reason for his expectations. The slender corsair was now barely halfway through the strait, making laborious headway. The Turanians, seeing their victim as good as caught, shouted with glee.

Dismay reigned among the pirate crew. Their progress was slow, and the Hyrkanian ships were closing in with every stroke, like hawks plummeting down upon a dove. Rolf stood silent, with the taciturnity of the northern barbarian, but Artus pleaded with his captain:

"Captain, the Hyrkanians will reach us long before we emerge! We stand no chance. We cannot maneuver in this narrow way, and their rams will splinter us like an eggshell. Could we not warp her ashore with the boats? We might put up a fight in the jungle. Tarim! We must do something!"

Conan, his calm unruffled, pointed at the oncoming war galleys. They were indeed a formidable sight. In the lead came the *Scimitar* with white water boiling up around her bow and her ten-foot bronze ram. She seemed a very angel of doom, descending in swift anger upon the wrongdoer. Close behind followed her sister, only a little less imposing.

"A pretty sight, by Ishtar," said Conan calmly. "Good speed, too. The slave drivers must be plying their whips with vigor. A heavy ship, that foremost one. Three or four times our weight."

His voice changed its tone from light banter to stern efficiency. "What are your soundings now?"

"Five fathoms, captain, and slowly increasing. We have passed the throat of the shallows. A wonder we did not scrape our bottom off!"

"Good! I knew we should get through. Now look at our pursuers!"

The *Scimitar*, bearing down upon her prey at full speed, suddenly stopped dead. A cracking of timbers and snapping of cordage resounded between the islands. Cries of dismay rent the air as the mast snapped off at the base and toppled, shrouding the decks in folds of canvas. The oars began backing to get her off, but her speed at the time of grounding had been too great. The unseen sandbank held her fast like a clutching octopus.

The other galley was a little more fortunate. Her captain was a man of decision and, when the leading vessel struck, he promptly ordered the oars to back water. But the oars were unevenly applied in the confusion and the galley veered to port toward the shore. She was saved from the cliffs only by another sandbank, into which she plowed deeply. Boats were launched and lines paid out to prepare for the arduous task of warping her afloat.

The throng on the deck of the corsair howled, shook their weapons, and made uncomplimentary gestures at the Turanians. They cheered Conan, and even the pessimistic shipmaster voiced his frank esteem.

"Those galleys will be days in getting afloat," said Artus. "I doubt the bigger one will ever sail again; her bottom must be half stove in.

"So, captain, whither do we sail? Khoraf, where the slavers put in with the fairest women of the South? Rhamdan, where the great caravan road ends?"

Conan's voice was tinged with scorn as he swept the throng with his ice-blue glance. "We have Turanian ships here, my friends. We have not escaped Yezdigerd; we have caught him in a trap! I promised you a feasting of swords. You shall have it." He paused, looking upward. "The wind freshens; we are coming out of lee. Set a course to round the larboard island!"

Eager hands sprang to the lines as all realized the full genius of Conan's planning.

King Yezdigerd paced the poop of his shattered flagship in blazing anger. Some of it he vented upon the seaman at the sounding post and the steersman, by having both beheaded forthwith. There was no immediate danger of sinking, for the hull had settled firmly upon the reef. But the hold had quickly filled with water from many sprung seams, indicating that the ship could probably never be saved. And the trick played upon the king by the escaping pirate infuriated his always irascible temper.

"I will hunt that dog to the ends of the earth!" he shouted. "The whole thing smacks of that devil Conan. I'll warrant he is aboard. Will Khogar never get his cursed tub afloat?"

Thus he raged while work progressed on the *Khoralian Star*. As the long day wore on, the crews slowly coaxed the ship off the sandbank by inches, by tugging and having with the ships' boats. The captain of the *Star* was deeply preoccupied with directing this work when his attention was drawn by the warning cry of the lookout. The man's voice was shrill with excitement, and his hands waved frantically.

Rounding the point, her yellow sail billowing majestically, came the ship they had expected to be in full flight. Sleek and beautiful she came. Her bulwarks and shrouds were lined with eager corsairs. Faintly, their mocking challenges reached the Turanians' ears, like the cries of faraway demons in Hell.

Straight for the helpless *Khoralian Star* she bore like a striking eagle. She rammed a ship's boat, cutting it in two and sending splinters and bodies flying. Then she shortened her sail, made a quick turn, and in an instant lay board and board with her prey. Grappling hooks bit into Turanian wood, and a rain of arrows preceded the yelling, murderous host that surged over the gunwales.

The Turanians fought bravely. Surprised by their enemy, yet their captain got them into a semblance of order. The corsairs swept the lower deck, littering the planks with corpses. But they were checked by a blast of arrows from the poop, where the Turanian soldiery were drawn up behind a bristling hedge of spears. Only a moment they checked their attack. Then they swept on irresistibly, led by their mail-clad barbarian captain, who shattered helmets and severed limbs left and right with an ease that seemed magical.

The Turanians could not stand against these hardened fighters, led by the ferocious Cimmerian. A vicious swipe of Conan's broadsword opened a breach in the spear hedge. The bloodthirsty horde swarmed over the poop, scattering the Hyrkanians like chaff.

The captain, knowing that his only chance of saving his ship lay in slaying the pirate leader, sprang to meet Conan. Their blades clashed in a circular dance of steel. But the Turanian could not master the swordcraft of Conan, veteran from a thousand battlefields. The sharp edge of the Turanian's yataghan shaved a raven lock from the Cimmerian's ducking head; then the heavy broadsword smashed into the captain's mailed side. Khogar sank down dying, his rib cage caved in.

The fight went out of the Turanian soldiery as their captain fell. Cries for quarter were heard. The men flung down their arms in clanking heaps.

Conan surveyed the scene with grim satisfaction. He had lost a score of men, but he had captured the only navigable ship at his enemy's disposal. Several of the pirate crew were already at work striking the fetters from the slaves' ankles. They shouted for joy as they found long-lost friends among them. Others herded the captive Turanians into custody below.

While a prize crew continued the labor of freeing the vessel, the pirate ship cast off. Her decks were jammed, for her own crew was augumented by scores of freed and hastily-armed galley slaves. She headed straight for the bigger prize.

In a tavern in Onagrul, a secret stronghold of the Vilayet pirates, loud voices called for more wine. The cool clear liquid poured into old Artus' cup as the ears of the throng itched for more of his tales. The grizzled shipmaster washed down the draught in thirsty gulps. Satisfied, he wiped his lips upon the back of his hand and took in the crowd of listeners with a glance.

"Aye, lads, you should have been there! Great and glorious was the fighting as we took the first one. Then we swept down upon Yezdigerd's *Scimitar*. We must have seemed like very devils out of Hell to them, but they were ready for us. They severed the lines of our grapnels with swords and axes, until our archers blasted them back from the rail and we warped in to their side by mighty efforts. We laid her board and board, and every man among us was fired with killing lust.

"Conan was the first aboard her. The Turanians closed in about him in a circle of swords, but he slashed at them so savagely that they gave way. Then we all came in a rush, and the fighting was fast and furious. The Turanians were all well-trained and hardened fighters, Yezdigerd's household troops, fighting under the eye of their king. For a moment the outcome was precarious, in spite of the ferocity of Conan, who smashed Turanian mail and arms like rotten wood. They stood in perfect unity, and our attacks recoiled from their massed ranks like bloody waves from a rock-bound shore.

"Then came a cry of triumph, for some of us had jumped down among the galley slaves, slain the overseers, and struck the chains from the rowers' ankles. The slaves surged up on the deck like a horde of lost souls. They snatched whatever weapons they could find from the corpses. Their hatred of their masters must have run deep. Heedless of their own lives, they drove into the Turanian ranks, shouldering us aside. Some flung themselves forward to be spitted upon Hyrkanian swords and spears, while others climbed over their corpses to strangle Turanians with their bare hands. I saw a giant galley slave use a Hyrkanian's body as a club, knocking his foes to the deck, before sinking down with a dozen arrows in his body.

"Confusion reigned. The glittering ranks wavered. Conan yelled a weird battle cry and flung himself into the press. We followed, determined to win or die.

"After that, red hell reigned. In a bloody tidal wave we swept the ship from stem to stern with steel. We scattered the foe like chaff before the wind of our swords, and the scuppers were choked with blood.

"Conan was terrible as a tiger. His broadsword struck like a thunderbolt. Corpses were scattered about him like wheat stalks before the sickle. He plunged in where the fighting was thickest, and always his advent spelled doom for the Hyrkanians. With all his savage passion, he moved toward the poop where Yezdigerd himself stood bellowing orders, surrounded by his picked men.

"Conan smote their ranks like a charging elephant. Men went down beneath his sword like dolls. Then a cry of rage came from Yezdigerd, and the king himself rushed to meet him. I think Yezdigerd must have missed him before then, as his surprise was patent to all. Savage curses streamed from his lips as they engaged.

" 'I saw your hand in this, Cimmerian cur!' he screamed. 'By Erlik, now you shall reap your deserts! Die, barbarian dog!'

"He aimed a terrific stroke at Conan's head. No ordinary man could have avoided or stopped that swift and powerful blow, but Conan is superior to a dozen ordinary men. With a jarring impact, he parried it in a flashing movement too quick for the eye to follow."

" 'Die yourself, jackal of Turan!' he thundered. For an instant they struck and parried like lightning, while the rest of us stopped fighting to watch. Then a mighty blow shattered Yezdigerd's shield and made him drop his shield arm. In one lightning sweep, Conan smote the bearded head from the king's giant body, which crumpled to the deck."

"After that, the Turanians surrendered meekly

117

enough. We did not get many prisoners, for the swords had taken too heavy a toll. A bare half of our original two hundred were left standing, but we had captured or slain three hundred of the Hyrkanian dogs."

He gulped down more wine and held out his cup for a refill. During the pause, a hearer asked: "What about the Turanian *yedka?* What became of her?"

Artus' brows clouded and he gave a visible shudder. "That was the strangest event of that memorable day. We were binding up wounds and herding prisoners, when the sun seemed to cloud over and a chill of doom fell upon us. The water swirled blackly about our ships. Wind moaned in the rigging like the lament of a lost soul, though we were under the lee of a cliff.

"Someone cried and pointed up. In the sky appeared a black dot, growing swiftly larger. At first it looked like a bird or bat. Then it grew to a fantastic, horrible shape, manlike but winged. With a rush of vast leatherly wings it swooped to the poop deck, uttering a shrill cry that smote our hearts like death.

"At that cry, the woman of Maypur stepped from the poop cabin, which none of us had yet entered. In the wink of an eye, the monster snatched her up and bore her off, flapping heavily over the oily waters of the channel. In a few seconds both were out of sight, and the sun shone once again.

"We stared at one another, white-faced. Everybody asked his neighbor what had happened. Had the fiend stayed, I am sure we should have all leaped into the sea to escape it, though it was gone so quickly that we had no time for panic. Even Conan looked shaken and pale.

" 'I have seen that thing before,' he muttered, but he would not explain. Some of us surmised that the devil had come to drag Thanara off to the hell of Erlik's

118

worshipers. But others, who had been standing close to her when the creature swooped upon us, said that she showed no fear of it, but rather eagerness, as if she had summoned it herself.

"At last Conan shook himself like one coming out of a daze and bellowed orders to strip the slain of valuables and pitch the corpses over the side, even the body of the king. All he would say of the abduction of Thanara was:

"'Let the damned hussy escape with her bogeyman. I do not war upon women, though I would have striped her hide for her treachery.'

"And that was the end of the matter. We burned the grounded galley and sailed the other one hither."

"And where is Conan?" cried another listener. "Why is he not here to tell us tales of his adventures himself? Will he return as our leader to sweep the Turanians from the sea?"

"Alas, no! The Cimmerian ordered the ships to make straight for the eastern shore. He said he was on a vital mission. He had paused here only to settle his old score with Yezdigerd. One of the slaves we freed was a Khitan. Conan remained with him for hours, squatting in conversation. They talked of far lands beyond the Himelias. If Khitai be his goal, he must seek some really fabulous treasure. Otherwise, who would be so mad as to try for those lands beyond the sunrise?"

"Why took he not a score of sea rovers with him?"

"That is another mystery. He swore he had taken an oath to journey alone, and that his goal would be unattainable otherwise.

"We landed him on the eastern shore, and the farewell between him and Rolf the northerner was short and manly. The crew in their sorrow began chanting a sea dirge, until he lifted his mighty voice to curse us to silence. We watched him disappear behind a sand dune on his way to unknown perils.

"Rolf is our captain now, and an abler one is not to be found barring Conan. For Conan will always remain the greatest captain of them all, even when Vilayet Sea has become a desert waste and the stars have fallen from the heavens. I drink his health, and may his quest be successful!"

The toast was drunk in a silence oddly out of place in a pirates' tavern.

6. Treason in the East

"AND HOW fares Her Royal Highness, the Devi?" Conan asked the fat taverner as he sat guzzling a goblet of the scented Shirakman wine of Vendhya. Trusting to the disguise of his Kshatriyan garb, he had ventured within its doors to slake his thirst not only for drink but also for knowledge of this alluring woman, whose empire he had saved. Old memories rushed into his mind. There was a faraway look in his icy blue eyes as he listened.

Although the tavern was almost empty, the rasping voice of its owner took on a cautious note as he bent forward to whisper into the Cimmerian's ear.

"Ah, the Devi rules with a wise and firm hand, though she has no consort to stand by her side and uphold her. But the nobility say the throne needs a warlike spirit. It is even whispered that her cousin Chengir Khan has an eye for the supreme power and also for herself. Hitherto she has repulsed his wooing, but public sentiment will soon force her to decide. The dynasty must be carried on, and Yasmina must do her duty to the realm."

The stout Vendhyan cast a swift glance through the open door. Heavy steps and the clank of weapons were heard as a troop swung by, bucklers on their arms and spears on their mailed shoulders. With professional discipline, the soldiers halted at their officer's command. Their scarred old *ghebra* stepped

121

into the tavern. His swift glance took in everybody, halting for an instant on Conan, then completing its circle back to the host.

Stepping up to the counter, the officer spoke in a whisper with the taverner. A couple of dusty bottles passed over the worn boards into the silken sack in his hand. His business concluded, he stepped out with long strides and barked a command. His detachment took up their measured step again.

Conan cast an indifferent glance after the troop as their steps receded. His head was full of Yasmina, alone in her palace, ruling the realm without the support of a consort. He shrugged. The internal affairs of Vendhya were not his present business.

He had, rather, better look to his own problems. Tomorrow he would be on his way east, toward the farther reaches of the Himelians, and for that long trek he should be well rested. His colossal frame could endure hardships unimaginable to a civilized man, but on dangerous missions his instincts prompted him to rest when he could, like a carnivore on a long hunt.

"Taverner!" rumbled Conan. "Have you a room for the night? I am near done with fatigue. These desert trips take the sap out of a man."

The Eastern night lay like a hot, caressing, silken blanket over the city of Ayodhya. Stars glittered in diamond splendor against the black sky, and the sickle of the waning moon rode in the west. Torches and candles flared. From bright-lit palaces sounded laughter and music and the patter of dancing girls' feet, while out of dimly illuminated temples rang the austere tones of golden cymbals and the soft massed voices of worshipers' choirs.

Conan awoke suddenly, with muscles poised like

122

springs for instant action. He had heard a fumbling at the door of his room. He had lain stretched full-length upon the bed, naked but for his silken breeks, spurning bedclothes in the sultry night. Now he rose noiselessly, sword in hand, alert as a wolf.

The latch was slowly and cautiously depressed. As the door began to open, Conan hid himself behind it. A veiled and robed figure of small stature, dim in the starlight, furtively entered. It halted uncertainly as if astonished to find the room empty.

Conan listened with sensitive ears. He could hear no sound outside. Clearly, the mysterious visitor had come alone. His purpose was unknown to Conan. Any Vendhyan recognizing Conan would have brought the whole municipal guard with him. Many Kshatriyas had not forgotten the marauding hill chief of Ghor, though it had been years since he had led his hairy hordes down from the hills to pillage.

Conan did not intend this situation to remain enig-matic any longer than necessary. Swinging the door silently to with a push of his big hand, he took a stealthy step forward. Like a flash, his hand was over the mouth of the intruder, who was borne down upon the bed like a child despite desperate resistance. Two frightened eyes looked up into Conan's as he hissed:

"Why are you here in my room? Talk, you! But hush your voice!"

He removed his hand from the mouth of the cap-tive and tore away the veil over the face. To his glance was revealed the full lips and straight, nar-row nose of a Vendhyan woman. In a voice like the silver chimes of a temple gong, she spoke:

"I came to fetch you to my mistress. She has learned of your coming and is anxious to see you. Don your clothes and we will be on our way. Make haste!"

Conan's eyes narrowed with suspicion. "Why this cursed haste, girl! Can't your lady let a man sleep in peace? Why not meet me tomorrow?"

"In the day, many people at my mistress' palace would know Conan of Ghor. She does not wish you torn in twain between wild elephants."

Conan was instantly on guard. "Conan of Ghor, eh? Who knows me here? Who is she? What does she want."

"I cannot tell you. But this she said ere I left the palace: 'If he hesitates, tell him the Galzai girl of Mount Yimsha would repay him for the clothes he once gave her.'"

Yimsha! Conan's thoughts wandered back thirteen years, to the momentous days when he had assaulted the evil wizards of the Black Circle, and how he had once provided a girl with clothes bought (at sword's point, true, but still with coin) from a Galzai girl on her way to the well. The girl he had outfitted was Yasmina herself!

"So your mistress is the Devi?" he growled. "Why didn't you say so in the first place?"

"Aye, the Devi bids you come. Now hurry!"

With practiced speed, Conan dressed and armed himself. The girl silently opened the door and peered out. Then, with a gesture, she motioned to Conan. The twain slipped noiselessly down the stairs and out into the hot night.

Their route was devious and twisting. Evidently there was truth in the rumors of intrigue that Conan had heard in the tavern, for his guide often cast quick glances over her shoulder. Many times she turned into narrow, cobbled lanes, darker than night itself, as if to shake off pursuers.

Once, in such a lane, a huge dog with glowing eyes and slavering jaws sprang upon them from a door-

124

way. The ripping thrust of the Cimmerian's dagger stretched him lifeless in the gutter. Another time, a knot of ragged men appeared at the end of the street, barring their exit. Conan's white-toothed smile and slap at the hilt of his sword sent them scurrying. No other disturbance barred their way.

Soon their journey ended. They stood before the high, crenelated wall around the royal palace. Its lofty towers reared narrow pinnacles against the sky; the smell of exotic flowers and fruit from the gardens within reached their nostrils. The girl scanned the surface of the wall. At last she pressed two places on it at the same time. Without a sound, a section swung inward, revealing a dimly-lit corridor.

Enjoining Conan to silence with a finger upon her lips, she led the way. The secret door swung noiselessly to behind him, and he followed her swift step along the corridor, hand on hilt. He was sure that Yasmina meant him no harm, or she would not have chosen this mode of fetching him, but his barbarian instincts kept him on guard.

They went up a stone staircase, then along more dim corridors, until at last the girl stopped before a door and peered through a small hole set at eye's height. She pulled a lever, and the door opened. They entered.

"Wait here, my lord," she said, "and I will tell my mistress that you are here."

She hurried from the room, wispy garments fluttering. Conan shrugged and let his eyes wander round the chamber.

Replete with the riches of an Eastern ruler it was, with silken hangings, golden cups and ornaments, and rich embroidery strewn with precious stones, yet its luxury was tempered by the quality of exquisite taste. That it was a woman's boudoir was evident from the vanity table with its costly Turanian mirror. It was strewn with jars of jade, gold, and silver, holding ointments and salves prepared by the most skilled cosmeticians of the East. Femininity also showed itself in the splendor of the great bed, with its opaque silken hangings and canopy of gold-worked Shemitish cloth.

Conan nodded in curt appreciation. Though he was a hardened warrior, yet his days as a king had taught him to find pleasure in beautiful surroundings. His thoughts were interrupted by a sound at his back. Wheeling, he half drew his sword; then he checked himself.

It was Yasmina. When he had first met her, she had been in the first flower of womanhood—hardly twenty as he remembered. Now, thirteen years later, she was a mature woman. The sharp wit that had enabled her to hold the throne still shone from her eyes, but her clinging silken garments revealed that her girlish figure had bloomed into a woman's desirable body. And that body was of such beauty that poets grew famous by describing it; it would have fetched over a thousand talars on the auction block at Sultanapur. Yasmina's beautiful face was suffused with happiness as she stopped three steps from him, arms half opened, murmuring:

"My hill chieftain! You have come back!"

Conan's blood pounded in his temples as he covered the distance between them in one mighty stride and took her in his arms. As her supple body pressed warmly against his, she whispered:

"We shall be undisturbed, my chieftain. I have sent away the guards for the night. The entrance to this room is locked. Love me, my chieftain! For thirteen years I have longed for the feel of your arms around me. I have not been happy since we parted after the battle in Femesh Valley. Hold me in your arms, and let this be a night that neither of us shall ever forget!"

In another part of the palace, five men sat in a richly furnished room. Ever and anon they sipped from golden goblets as they listened to the tall, swarthy man.

"Now is the time!" he said. "Tonight! I have just learned that Yasmina has sent away the score of soldiers who usually guard her chambers. A woman's whim, no doubt, but it will serve us well!"

"My lord Chengir," one of the others interrupted, "is it really necessary to slay the Devi? I have fought Turanian squadrons on the border and hewed my way out of hillmen's ambushes, but I like not the thought of striking down a woman in cold blood."

The tall man smiled. "Neither do I, Ghemur, but it is necessary for the kingdom of Vendhya. The blood of the realm needs renewal. There must be new conquests to augment our power. The Devi has weakened the fiber of the country by her peaceful rule. We, a race of conquering warriors, now waste our time building dams and roads for the filthy lower castes! Nay, she must die. Then I, as successor to the throne, will lead the Kshatriyas to new conquests. We will carve out a new empire in blood in Khitai, in Uttara Kuru, in Turan. We'll sweep the hillmen from the Himelias in a red flood. The East shall shake and totter to our thunder! Day and night, camel trains laden with spoil shall pour into Ayodhya. Are you with me?"

Four curved swords slid halfway out of their gold-worked sheaths, and the clamor of the generals' assent was a loud murmur.

The prince waved them to silence. "Not so loud, sirs.

Remember that nearly all are loyal to Yasmina. Few have our foresight. Should we attempt an open revolt, the troops and the people would tear us to pieces. But should she die by secret assassination . . . Of course I, as her cousin and heir, would diligently search for the malefactors. Perhaps we could execute a couple of scapegoats—after cutting out their tongues. After a suitable time of mourning, I shall gather my army and strike to the north and to the east. My name will be lauded in history with our great conquerors of old!"

His voice rang high with excitement and his eyes shone. With an imperious gesture, he rose. "Arm yourselves, gentlemen. Don your masks. We go to Yasmina's chambers by a secret passage. Our duty to the kingdom will be performed within the hour!"

Five black-masked nobles filed out of the room on their way to cut the throat of a defenseless woman.

The faint light of the stars sifted into the queen's bedchamber, as Conan awoke for the second time that night. His sharp ears caught a soft, almost inaudible sound. Any ordinary man would have muttered sleepily, attributed the disturbance to rats or bad dreams, turned over, and gone back to sleep.

Not so Conan! Instantly wide awake, he investigated. His animal instincts were on edge. As his right hand sought the hilt of his sword and drew it noiselessly from its shagreen scabbard, his left parted the hangings to get a view of the room. Yasmina lay sleeping, a faint smile on her beautiful lips.

It needed not the glint of steel in the hands of five dark figures, faintly outlined in the starlight, to tell Conan that here was deadly danger. Masked men did not nightly invade their queen's chamber with

128

kindly intentions. Catlike, he crouched on the balls
of his feet, sword in hand, rage in his heart.

The assassins stole closer, readying their daggers for
the strokes that would seat a new ruler on the throne
of Vendhya. One was already plucking at the
hangings of the royal bed.

Conan went into action with blurring speed. Like
a maddened tiger he sprang. The nearest man was
down, disemboweled, before the others recovered from
their shock. His sword flashed quick as a striking
cobra. With a crash, the helmet and head of another
were cloven to the chin. Conan kicked the corpse
against the others, breaking their charge, while
parrying a cut against his legs by one who had
dodged the human missile. With a terrific backhanded
swipe, he smote the sword arm from the man's body.
The limb fell jerking to the floor, while the assassin
sank down in a heap.

Conan stormed against the remaining two. With
flashing sabers, they fought for their lives under the
maddened onslaught of the naked Cimmerian. Red
fury blazed in Conan's eyes as he rained mighty
strokes upon their frantic parries, circling them to
keep them from getting on opposite sides of him.

"Murder a woman sleeping in her bed, will you?"
he snarled. "Cowards! Jackals! Any treacherous Stygian is a fair fighter compared to you! But no blood
shall be spilt tonight but yours, curs!"

Conan's blade flickered like a shaft of deadly light.
A terrific slash shore off the head of one of his masked
adversaries, with the ferocity of the Cimmerian's attack backed the single one remaining against the
wall. Their swift blows and parries shaped a glittering, ever-changing pattern of steel in the starlight.

Yasmina, now fully awake, stood beside her bed,

watching with bated breath. Suddenly she cried out in terror, as Conan slipped in the blood on the floor and fell across one of the corpses.

The Vendhyan assailant sprang forward, unholy glee in his black eyes. He raised his sword. Conan struggled to rise. Suddenly, the mouth of his foe flew open. He teetered, dropping his sword, and fell with a choking gurgle. Behind was revealed the naked, supple form of Yasmina. Between the shoulders of the dead Kshatriya protruded the hilt of the dagger she had driven home in the nick of time to save her lover.

Conan slashed himself free from the entangling folds of a mantle and rose. From head to foot he was covered with blood, but his blue eyes blazed with their old unquenchable fire.

"Lucky for me you were quick with your sticker, girl! But for you, I should have kept these gentlemen company in Hell by now. Crom, but it was a good fight!"

Her first reply was one of feminine anxiety. "You bleed, my chieftain! Come with me to the bathroom, and we will dress your wounds."

"It's theirs, all but a couple of scratches," grunted Conan, wiping the blood off with the turban cloth of one of the dead assasins. "Small price to pay to thwart these scoundrels."

"I praise the gods you were with me, or they would have succeeded." The Devi's voice was vibrant with emotion. "Never have I dreamed that assassination threatened me! The people deem my rule just, and I have the backing of the army and most of the nobility. Maybe Yezdigerd of Turan has sent emissaries as masked murderers to my chambers."

"Yezdigerd won't bother you again," muttered the

Cimmerian. "He's dead. I slew him on his own ship. Unmask them!"

The Devi tore the mask from the face of the man she had knifed, then recoiled in amazement and horror. "Chengir! My own cousin! Oh, treachery, black treachery and power madness! Heads shall roll for this tomorrow!"

She shook her raven tresses and turned her dark, liquid eyes on the inscrutable face of the Cimmerian. "I know now that I need a consort. Rule Vendhya with me, Conan! Tomorrow we'll announce our bethrothal; within a month there will be nuptial feasts and ceremonies such as have not taken place in Vendhya for a hundred years! I love you, my chieftain!"

She embraced him hotly, straining with her vigorous, slim young body against his, covering his lips with kisses, until his senses swam. But he shook his head and thrust her gently from him. He held her at arm's length.

"Crom knows, lass, that you make a tempting offer," he rumbled. "Few women have I seen so beautiful as you, nor so wise. Any man blessed with your hand in marriage would count himself the favorite of a hundred gods. Ten years ago, when I was a wandering soldier of fortune, I would perhaps have accepted. Now I cannot. I have my own kingdom now, Aquilonia in the West, the mightiest realm in the world. But my queen has been stolen from me by an evil magician in Khitai, and I have sworn an oath to get her back. I should not be a man if I did not keep my vow. Marry one of your own people. They would rather be ruled by a king of their own blood. Tomorrow I ride for the Himelians."

There was misty tenderness and vast love in the

deep, brimming eyes of Yasmina as she regarded him. "The gods give happiness only to snatch it away. Mayhap that is as well, or life would be nothing but happiness, and we should lack the contrasts to know what real happiness means." Her eyes cleared, and a queer, half-whimsical smile played upon her lips. "You will go tomorrow. But there are several hours left until dawn. Let us spend them in a more profitable way than talking!"

They locked again in a fierce embrace, while the stars shone coldly upon the dead, glassy-eyed faces of the foiled assassins.

7. The Demon of the Snows

THE MAN slunk silently along the snow-covered trail. His body was bent forward; his eyes scanned the ground, and his nostrils widened like those of a hound on the scent. No man had ever before been where he now stalked; at least, none had been there and returned to tell about it. Mist-veiled and mysterious were the icy upper wastes of the mighty Himelian mountains.

Zelvar Af had been hunting alone when he happened upon the odd tracks in the snow. Wide, splayed footprints were pressed deeply down at distances of at least four feet, denoting the size of the creature that made them. Zelvar Af had never seen anything like them; but his memory stirred with the recollection of ghastly legends told in the thatched huts of the hill villages by white-bearded old men.

With primitive recklessness, Zelvar Af shrugged off the glimmerings of fear. True, he was alone and several days' journey from home. But was he not the foremost hunter of the Wamadzi? The double curve of his powerful Hyrkanian bow brought reassurance as he clutched it with his eyes searching. He moved cat-footed on the trail.

It was no manifestation of sound or sight that made him stop. The white slopes stretched upward before him in snowy magnificence. Other mighty ranges could be seen far off in jagged silhouette. No sign of life showed anywhere. But an icy, creeping feeling suddenly filled his mind—the feeling that something arisen from dreaful tales of horrible beings from dark borderlands. He wheeled in a flash, his brown hand whipping out his heavy Zhaibar knife.

His blood froze in his veins. His eyes opened in awful terror at the sight of the giant white shape that glided toward him over the snow. No features could be discerned in the white face of the horribly manlike figure, but its swift glide brought it straight to its petrified victim. With a scream of terror, Zelvar swung his blade. Then the icy embrace of the smothering white arms swept around him. Silence reigned again in the vast white reaches.

"By thunder, it is good to be among hillmen again!"

The words were stressed by a bang on the rough wooden table with a half-gnawed beef bone. A score of men were gathered in the big hut of the chief of the Khirgulis: chiefs from neighboring villages and the foremost men of the Khirguli tribe. Wild and fierce they were. Clothed in sturdy hillman's sheepskin tunics and boots, they had doffed the huge fur coats worn against the cold of the upper ranges, displaying the barbaric splendor of Bakhariot belts and ivory-and-gold tulwar hilts.

The commanding figure was, however, none of these fierce mountaineers. Conan the Cimmerian, in the place of honor, was the center of their attention. Long and varied was the tale he had told, for it was over a decade since his feet had last trod the winding paths of the Himelian crags.

"Yes, I think you will be little bothered by Turanians henceforth." Flashes coruscated in the blue depths of Conan's eyes as he told his recent experiences. "I

134

slew Yezdigerd on the deck of his flagship, as the blood of his men gushed round my ankles. His vast empire will be sundered and split by the feuds of Shahs and Aghas, as there is no successor to the throne."

The gray-bearded chief sighed. "We have seen little of the Turanians since the day you with your Afghulis and the Devi Yasmina with her Kshatriyas defeated their host in Femesh Valley. Nor have the riders of Vendhya bothered us; we keep a silent agreement of truce since that day, even refraining from raiding their caverns and outposts. I almost long for the old days of battle, when we rained stones upon their spired helmets and ambushed their mailed lancers from every cranny."

Conan smiled in reminiscence. But his thoughts dwelt on his recent visit to Vendhya. It was hard to push the picture of a slim, black-haired, tear-eyed woman out of his mind, as he remembered her standing on the palace wall, waving her silken veil as he thundered away toward the hazy mountains.

A portly, bearded chief cleared his throat. "We understand that you are on a pressing errand, Conan," he said. "But take our advice and go around the Talakman region. Strange and terrible things happen there, and it is whispered that the snow demons of the old myths are abroad again."

"What are these snow demons, that they send fear into the stout hearts of the men of Ghulistan?"

The chief bent lower and answered with a quaver in his voice. "Devils out of the nighted gulfs of the black abyss haunt the snowy reaches of Talakma. Men have been found with their bodies broken and mangled by something of terrible strength and ferocity. But the most horrible thing of all is that every corpse, no matter how recent, was frozen stiff to the core! Fingers and limbs are so brittle that they break of like icicles!"

"I thank you for the warning." Conan's voice was somber. "But I cannot pass around the Talakmas. It would cost me two months, and I must travel by the straightest path. My time is short."

Clamoring, they tried to dissuade him, but in vain. His stentorian voice beat upwards to tones of command, whereupon they all fell silent.

He rose heavily and went into the inner room to a bed covered with thick furs, while his companions lingered, shaking their heads and muttering in fearful tones.

The wind howled sadly as Conan made his way across the snowy vastness. Gusts flung biting snow into his weather-beaten face, and the icy blasts pierced his thick fur coat. Slung from his shoulders was his pack, crammed with supplies for the long trek over the cold wastes, dried meat and coarse bread. His breath stood out in a long plume from his nostrils.

For days he had been upon his way, traversing the snows with the easy, long-limbed hillman's stride that eats up the mountainous miles. At night he had slept in primitive snow caves, dug with the crude, broad-bladed shovel carried for the purpose, and at day-break he hurried on again. Chasms gaped across his path. Sometimes his muscular legs took them in a running broad jump. Sometimes he had to make a wide detour around the end of the chasm, or lower himself into the deeps with his climbing rope and scramble up the other side.

The snows were unbroken and almost deserted by living things. Once a hungry snow leopard charged him, but he broke the carnivore's attack with a ripping thrust of his Zhaibar knife. The animal tumbled to the ground, choking out its life in convulsions. He left it there to lie forever in the eternal cold.

As the snow-laden wind lessened, he wiped the icy particles from his brows, paused, and looked about him. Behind stretched the interminable plains of snow, broken by yawning abysses and jutting peaks, which lost themselves in the distance. Far in front, he dimly discerned the beginning of the downward slope of the mountains and the promise of an end to this gruelling leg of his journey.

Then his sharp blue eyes espied something else. With sudden curiosity, Conan moved forward to investigate. He paused, looking down at the odd footprints that had caught his attention. Unlike any spoor he had ever seen, they looked a little like the tracks of a bear. But no bear ever left footprints so large, without claw marks and with those curiously splayed toes. They must have been made recently, for the drifting snow had only partly filled them. They led close by a towering, mountainous mass of ice. Conan followed the trail, alert as a stalking panther.

Even the Cimmerian's lightning quickness failed to avoid the monstrous white form that suddenly hurtled upon him from above. He had a glimpse of shapeless limbs and horribly featureless head. Then he was flung to the ground with such violence that the breath was knocked out of his lungs.

Because of his quick reaction, the snaky arms had not wholly enveloped him. His body had half-twisted out of their descending grip, though they grabbed him in a vicelike clutch back and front.

He struggled madly to free his right hand and slash at his foe with the naked knife in his fist, but even his giant strength seemed like a babe's to the demoniac power of the monster. And then a horrible, featureless face bent forward, as if to stare straight into his eyes. An abysmal chill began to envelop his body, and he felt a deadly tugging at the borders of his mind. In that amorphous terror he saw mirrored the abysmal evil of the darker gulfs where slavering things dwell, preying on human souls. Forces tore at the roots of his reason; icy drops of sweat sprang out on his forehead.

A weaker man would have succumbed to the evil of this unknown and overwhelming power, but the civilized layer was only a thin coating over Conan's barbarian reflexes. His animal instincts rushed to the fore of his mind. The urge to self-preservation made his muscles contract in one mighty effort. With a tearing of fur and clothing, he ripped his left hand free of the constraining whiteness and smashed into the blank visage facing him.

At the first blow, the monster uttered a shrill, ululating cry and slackened its grip.

The ring!

The ring of Rakhamon, the gift of Pelias, with unknown powers of magic and sorcery, that Conan carried! A deadly weapon against this waif of the icy darkness, that tore men's souls from their bodies to eternal damnation and left them broken and frozen on the snows!

Conan struck again, and now the ululation changed to a shrill shriek as the white horror flung itself backward to escape the terror of the ring. With savage glee, Conan lunged after it. Now he was the attacker! Using the sharp rhomboid points of the ring as a weapon, he ripped savagely into the white form.

There was a shrill bellow from the facial region of the creature. It fled over the snow, white ichor dripping from its wounds, while Conan pursued it like an avenging spirit.

Its steps carried it to the brink of an icy chasm, where it paused, at bay, tottering and trembling. Mercilessly, Conan slashed with his ringed fist at its body. With a weird shriek it staggered backward. For a moment it fought for balance on the edge; then the icy crust gave way. With a long-drawn wail it hurtled downwards into the darkness of the abyss.

Conan shook himself like a wolf-dog after the hunt. "Pelias gave me a powerful bauble indeed," he mumbled. "A pox on these snow demons! That one has been cast back to its hellish haunts, anyway. Now I'd better hurry, if I am to reach the downward slopes tomorrow."

8. The Dragon of Khitai

It was the twenty-fifth day since he had crossed the Khitan border.

The arid, sandy lands bordering the vast Wuhuan Desert, unpeopled save for straggling bands of weather-beaten nomads, had been relieved by vast bogs and marshes. Waterfowl whirred up in clouds from pools of stagnant water. Red-eyed, ill-tempered marsh buffalo splashed and snorted in the tall reeds. Swarms of biting insects hummed; tigers on the hunt uttered coughing roars. Conan needed all his swamp-craft, acquired in the Kushite jungles and the marshes fringing the Sea of Vilayet, to cross these inhospitable reaches, with the help of hand-made swamp shoes and improvised bamboo rafts.

When the fens ended, thick jungle began. This was not much easier to penetrate. Conan's heavy Zhaibar knife was at constant work cutting through dense undergrowth, but the iron muscles and dogged determination of the giant Cimmerian never flagged. These parts had once been rich and civilized, long ago when Western civilization was barely in its morning glow. In many places Conan found crumbling ruins of temples, palaces, and whole cities, dead and forgotten for thousands of years. Their empty window-holes stared blackly like the eye sockets of skulls in somber forgetfulness. Vines draped the worn and pitted statues of weird, pre-human gods. Chattering apes shrieked their displeasure at his intrusion into their green-mantled walls.

The jungle melted into rolling plains, where saffron-skinned herdsmen watched their flocks. Straight across this part of the land, across hills and valleys alike, ran the Great Wall of Khitai. Conan surveyed it grimly. With a thousand stout Aquilonian warriors, equipped with rams and catapults, he would soon breach this vast but static defense, by a lightning thrust ere help could come from other sections of the wall.

But he had no thousand soldiers with siege engines, and cross the Great Wall he must. One dark night, when the moon was veiled, he stole over by means of a rope, leaving a guardsman stunned by a blow on the helm. The grassy fields were traversed in the tireless, mile-devouring barbarian jog-trot, which enabled him to cover vast distances between rests.

The jungle soon began anew. Here, however, were signs of the passing of man, lacking in the other forests through which he had hewn a laborious way. Narrow paths were beaten through the undergrowth, though it massed as thickly as ever among the clustered bamboo stems on the sides. Vines festooned the trees; gay-feathered birds twittered. From far away came the snarl of a hunting leopard.

Conan slunk along the path like an animal born to jungle life. From the information he had gleaned from the Khitan slave freed after the sea fight on the Vilayet Sea, he deduced that he was now in the jungle bordering the city-state of Paikang. The Khitan had told him that it took eight days to cross this belt of forest. Conan counted on making it in four. Drawing upon his immense barbarian resources of vitality, he could undergo exertions unthinkable to other men.

Now his goal was to reach some settlement. The tale was that the forest folk lived in dread of Pai-kang's cruel ruler. Therefore Conan counted on finding friends who could furnish him with directions for reaching the city.

The eerie atmosphere of the bamboo jungle pressed down upon him with almost physical force. Unbroken and unexplored for thousands of years, save for narrow paths and small clearings, it seemed to hold the answers to the mysteries of aeons. An enigmatic aura of brooding enveloped the glossy, naked stems of the bamboo, which rose on every hand in jutting profusion. The esoteric traditions of this land reached back before the first fire was lit in the West. Vast and ancient was the knowledge hoarded by its philosophers, artisans, and sorcerers.

Conan shrugged off the depressing influence and gripped the hilt of his tulwar more firmly. His feet trod silently on the matting of moldering leaves. His faculties were sharpened and alert, like those of a wolf raiding into the lands of a foreign pack. There was a rustle among the half-rotten leaves. A great snake, slate-gray with a flaming red zigzag along its back, reared its head from its hiding place. It struck viciously, with bared and dripping fangs. At that instant, the steel in Conan's hand flashed. The tulwar's keen edge severed the head of the reptile, which writhed and twisted in its death throes. Conan grimly cleaned his blade and pressed on.

Then he halted. Stock-still he stood, ears sharpened to the utmost, nostrils widened to catch the faintest scent. He had heard the clank of metal and now could catch the sound of voices.

Swiftly but cautiously he advanced. The path

made a sudden turn a hundred paces further on. At this corner his sharp eyes sought the cause of the disturbance.

In a small clearing, two powerful yellow-skinned Khitans were trussing a saffron-hued girl to a tree. Unlike most of the Far Eastern folk, these men were tall and powerful. Their lacquered, laminated armor and flaring helmets gave them a sinister, exotic look. At their sides hung broad, curved swords in lacquered wooden scabbards. Cruelty and brutality were stamped on their features.

The girl twisted in their grip, uttering frantic pleas in the singsong, liquid Khitan tongue. Having learned more than a smattering of it in his youth, when he had served the king of Turan as a mercenary, Conan found he could understand the words. The captive's slant-eyed face was of a startling oriental beauty.

Her pleading had no effect on her merciless captors, who continued their work. Conan felt his rage mounting. This was one of those cruel human sacrifices which he had tried to stamp out in the western world but which were still common in the East. His blood boiled at the sight of this manhandling of a defenseless girl. He broke from cover with a bull-like rush, sword out.

The crackling of the underbrush beneath the Cimmerian's feet reached the ears of the Khitan soldiers. They swung round towards the sound, and their eyes widened with unfeigned surprise. Both whipped out their swords and prepared to meet the barbarian's attack with arrogant confidence. They spoke no word, but the girl cried out:

"Flee! Do not try to save me! These are the best swordsmen in Khitai! They belong to the bodyguard of Yah Chieng!"

The name of his foe brought a greater fury to

Conan's heart. With slitted eyes, he struck the Khitans like a charging lion.

Unequalled as swordsmen in Khitai they may have been, but before the wrath of Conan they were like straws in the wind. The barbarian's blade whirled in a flashing dance of death before their astonished eyes. He feinted and struck, crushing armor and shoulder bone beneath the keen edge of his hard-driven tulwar. The first yellow man sank down, dying.

The other, hissing like a snake, exploded into a fierce attack. Neither fighter would give way. Their blades crashed ringingly together. Then the inferior steel of Khitai broke before the supple strength of the tulwar, forged from matchless Himelian ore by a Khirguli smith. Conan's blade ripped through the armor plate into the Khitan's heart.

With muted fear, the captive girl had followed the fight with widened eyes. When Conan broke from cover, she thought him one of her friends or relatives, bent upon a mad attempt to rescue her.

Now she saw that he was a *cheng-li*, a white-skinned foreigner from the legendary lands west of the Great Wall and the Wuhuan Desert. Would he devour her alive, as legends averred? Or would he drag her back to his homeland as slave, to work chained in a filthy dungeon the rest of her life?

Her fears were soon allayed by Conan's friendly grin as he swiftly cut her bonds. His appreciative glance ran over her limbs, not with the air of a captor sizing up the value of a captive, but with the glance of a free man looking upon a free woman. Her cheeks were suffused with blood before his frank admiration.

"By Macha" he said, "I did not know they bred women this beautiful in the yellow lands! It seems I

144

should have visited these parts long ago!" His accent was far from perfect, but she had no difficulty in following the words.

"Seldom do white strangers come to Khitai," she answered. "Your arrival and victory were timed by the gods. But for you, those two" (she indicated the corpses) "would have left me helpless prey to the terror Yah Chieng has let loose in the jungle."

"I have sworn to settle my debt with that scoundrel," growled Conan. "It seems I have to settle yours at the same time. What is this jungle terror you speak of?"

"None has met it and lived to tell. Men say the archwizard has conjured up a monster out of forgotten ages, when fire-breathing beasts walked the earth and the crust shook with earthquakes and eruptions. He holds the land in abject terror of it, and human sacrifices are often demanded. The fairest women and ablest men are taken by his soldiers to feed the maw of the beast of terror."

"Meseems this is no healthy neighborhood," said Conan. "Though I fear not this monster of yours, I'd as lief not be hindered by it on my way to Paikang. Is your village far?"

Before she could answer, there was a heavy crashing in the undergrowth. The bamboo stems shook and swayed, and a hoarse bellow reached their startled ears. Conan gripped his hilt, a grim smile on his lips. The girl shrank behind his mighty frame. Tense as a tiger, the Cimmerian waited.

With a croaking growl, a giant, scaly form crashed through the undergrowth at the fringe of the clearing. Dimly seen in the darkness of the forest, the sunlight of the glade revealed its terrible form in full. Forty feet it measured from snout to spiked tail. Its short, bowed legs were armed with sharp, curved claws. Its jaws were gigantic, set with teeth beside which a sabertooth's fangs were puny. Mighty swellings at the sides of its head told of the great muscles that worked this awful engine of destruciton. Its scaly hide was of a repellant leaden hue, and its fetid breath stank of moldering corpses.

It stopped for a moment in the sunlight, blinking. Conan used the time for swift action.

"Climb that tree! He can't reach you there!" he thundered to the terror-frozen girl.

Stung to action, the girl followed his command, while the Cimmerian's attention was again engaged by the giant lizard. This was one of the most formidable antagonists he had ever faced. Amored knights, sword-swinging warriors, blood thirsty carnivores, and skulking poisoners—all were dwarfed by the menace of this giant engine of destruction rushing upon him.

But the foremost hunter of the Cimmerian hills, the jungles of Kush, and the Turanian steppes was not to be taken in one gulp. Conan stood his ground, lest, if he fled or climbed a tree, the dragon should turn its attention to the girl. Then, an instant before the mighty jaws would have closed about him, he sprang to one side. The impetus of the dragon's charge carried it crashing into the undergrowth, while Conan ran to a clump of bamboos.

More quickly than he expected, the monster, roaring and crashing, untangled itself from the thickets and returned to the attack. Conan saw that he could not hope to reach the tree in which the girl had taken refuge in time to escape those frightful jaws. The glossy tubes of the bamboo afforded no holds for climbing, and their stems would be snapped by a jerk of the monster's head. No safety lay that way.

Whipping out his Zhaibar knife, Conan chopped through the base of a slim stem of bamboo. Another cut, slantwise, sheared off its crown of leaves and left a glassy-sharp rounded point. With this improvised ten-foot lance, Conan charged his oncoming adversary.

He rammed the point between the gaping jaws and down the darkness of the gullet. With a mighty heave of his straining muscles, Conan drove the bamboo deeper and deeper into the soft internal tissues of the dragon. Then the jaws slammed shut, biting off the shaft a foot from Conan's hand, and a sidewise lunge of the head hurled Conan into a thicket twenty feet away.

The grisly reptile writhed in agony, uttering shrieks of pain. Conan dragged himself to his feet, feeling as if every muscle in his body had been torn loose from its moorings. His arm ached as he drew his tulwar, yet by sheer will power he forced his battered body into service. He stumbled forward, half-blinded by dust, but avoiding the thrashing tail and snapping jaws.

Grimly, he put his whole strength into one desperate lunge for the monster's eye. The blade went in like a knife through butter. The hilt was snatched from his grasp by the last convulsions of the dying beast. Again he was thrown to the ground, but with a final tremor, the hulk of his terrible foe subsided.

Conan gasped the dust-laden air, picked himself up, and limped toward the tree where huddled the girl.

"I must be growing old," he muttered between gasps "A little fight like that wouldn't have bothered me at all in the old days."

This was but the barbarian's naïve way of belittling his feat. He knew that no other man could have

147

done what he had just accomplished; nor could he have succeeded but for luck and the ways of fate. He roared hoarsely:

"Come down, lass! The dragon ate more bamboo than was good for him. Now lead me to your village. I shall need help from you in return."

9.   The Dance of the Lions

SMOKE OF THE yellow lotus spiraled wispily upward in the dim-lit bamboo hut. Like clutching tentacles, it writhed in fragrant streamers toward the chimney-hole in the ceiling, curling from the mouthpiece of carven jade ending the silken hose of the elaborate, gold-bowled water-pipe on the floor and from the pursed and wrinkled lips of an old Khitan, sitting cross-legged on a reed mat.

His face was like yellowed parchment. Nearly fourscore years must have weighed upon his shoulders. Yet there was an air of youthful energy and command about him, coupled with calm and serenity of thought. He held the mouthpiece in his left hand, puffing slowly in sybaritic enjoyment of the narcotic fumes. Meanwhile, his sharp black eyes studied the big, black-haired, white-skinned man in front of him, who sat upon a low stool and wolfed down the *shi-la* rice stew placed before him by the girl he had saved.

She was now clad in a chastely high-necked jacket and embroidered trousers, which set off her golden complexion and large, deep, slanted eyes to advantage. With her lustrous hair combed into a complex coiffure, it was a startling transformation from the tousle-headed, half-naked, frightened girl whom he had rescued from men and monster. But he recalled the clasp of her hot arms during an hour of rest in the jungle, when she had given him a woman's reward, freely and willingly, in a burst of Oriental passion that needed no torch to inflame his desires.

One day and one night they had journeyed, resting only when the girl needed it. When she was utterly spent, he flung her across his broad shoulders, while his untiring legs pounded along. At last the path widened into a clearing. A dozen bamboo huts with shingled roofs were grouped near a brook, where fish splashed in silvery abundance. Wooden-featured, yellow-skinned men emerged with swords and bows at the intrusion, only to utter cries of joy and shouts of welcome to this savior of a daughter of their village.

For it seemed that these people were outcasts of noble blood, who had fled from the tyranny of Yah Chieng the Terrible. Now they dwelt on the edge of life, fearing every moment to be wiped out by a cohort of the sorcerer's dreaded swordsmen.

Wiping his mouth with the appearance of surfeit and taking a last draft from the bowl of yellow rice wine, Conan listened to the words of his host.

"Aye, mighty was the clan of Kang, of which I, Kang Hsiu, am the head," he said. "And fairest of all the city-states of northern Khitai was purple-towered Paikang. Hosts of glittering warriors shielded us from the warlike ambitions of Shu-chen to the north and Ruo-gen to the south. The lands were rich and the crops always plentiful. I dwelt in the palace in Paikang surrounded by all the splendor and culture of our ancient civilization.

"Then came the Accursed One. On one dark night his hordes swept up from the southeast like a destroying blaze. Our armies were wiped out by his foul arts. They were engulfed by earthquakes, devoured by magical fire, or smitten with the dry plague. Our sword arm was withered, and his hellhounds made free with our beautiful city. Paikang was sacked in fury and blood, in thunderous fires and unnamable atrocities. I, my family, and some of my retainers fled on fast camels. Through many perils we found this refuge. I doubt if Yah Chieng knows of us, or he would surely have wiped us out by now. Kang Lou-dze, my daughter here, was captured by his swordsmen while visiting a village several miles from here. No hunters ever come to this hidden place.

"It would seem that our plight is hopeless. We are but a handful, to face magical might and thousands of well-armed soldiers. Still, the people, whom he is grinding to poverty by his taxes and extortions, long for the bygone days of serenity, freedom, and wealth. They would rise if given the chance. But the iron heels of Yah Chieng's generals press upon their necks. His swordsmen swagger the streets of the cities like conquerors, with whips in their hands.

"So it has been for a score of years, and our hope dwindles. It would die but for the prophecy, in which we have put all our faith during these years of terror."

Conan had listened silently, but curiosity now prompted a question. "The memories of many happenings lie crowded in my mind. But this prophecy? What of it?"

"My wife, the mother of Kang Lou-dze, was gifted with strange powers. She knew the calls of birds, and I have often seen the wild beasts of the jungle nuzzling her hands. When disaster struck, one of Yah Chieng's marauders found his way to her chamber and struck her down while she prayed to our gods. I was too late to save her, but as I stood with dripping blade over the body of her murderer, she beckoned to me from the floor where she lay in her blood, and whispered into my grief-stricken ear:

151

" 'My days are ended. Flee swiftly to save our family. Hide yourselves and wait. Despair not. For there will come from the west a conqueror such as you have never seen, with a great and noble heart. In his wrath he will crush the fiend like a snake under his heel. He will be a man of white skin and great strength, a king in his own land, and he will smite the usurper like a flaming thunderbolt. The gods are with him, and Paikang will once again—'

"In that instant her mouth filled with a rush of blood, and she died. Stricken as I was, I could not stay. I gathered my children, and my servants helped me to carry the younger ones through a secret passage.

"Through all these years we have waited for the white war lord. We have listened for rumors of his shining armies and hoped to see his pennon on the towers of Paikang. But only marauding nomads have come from the Great Desert, and our hope has dwindled with the years.

"Except for a troop of mercenaries that Yah Chieng captured last year, you are the first man with white skin and round eyes to come from the West during all this time, but the prophecy said our savior would be a king and a conqueror. You are alone, without armies or followers, and you wear the habit of the nomads.

"I am old, my days are numbered, and now I begin to despair for the fate of my people."

A broad smile split Conan's face. Thumping the floor, he boomed: "Who said I'm no king, old man? King I am, and king of the mightiest kingdom of the West, fair Aquilonia. Conquered it myself, I did, and strangled its tyrant on the throne with my own hands. White I am, and my strength has won me duels with professional stranglers. Do I not fit your prophecy?"

The old man looked up, eager and incredulous at

152

the same time. "Is this true, Conan? You are a king? Then the part I did not tell you is also true—for my beloved wife said that this would occur within twenty years of our defeat. The gods be praised! We shall have a feast of prayer and thanksgiving tonight. To-morrow we are at your command! Will you lead us?"

Conan's laugh was gusty. "Not so hotly, my friend! Even I, who have had my share of follies, am not so rash as to rush into the maw of this scoundrel with only a score of men. The gods help those who use their wits. We must lay our plans carefully."

Then his voice was drowned by the joyful shouts of the crowd that had gathered outside the hut, sum-moned by Kang Lou-dze. With sudden sobriety he accepted the humble adoration of these folk, whose sole hope of salvation he represented.

The high council of the Khitan village of outcasts was in session. The atmosphere inside the bamboo hut was rife with tension. Conan lolled on the floor mats, a beaker of wine in his hand, while his sharp blue eyes scrutinized his new allies. The air was thick with the lotus-scented smoke of water pipes.

"It will be no easy task to win entrance to the fiend's castle," said one tall, slant-eyed man, whose face was disfigured by a scar across his brow. "His cursed swordsmen guard it day and night, and there are his own unearthly powers in the bargain. The people have no arms, and a straightforward attack on the heavily-fortified citadel is out of the question with our scant force."

"You are right, Leng Chi," said the aged Kang Hsiu. "Stealth and trickery pave the road to success. And I know of only one way that might carry us there. In a week, Yah Chieng will give his annual, feast in celebration of the conquest of Paikang. The climax of this feast is always the Dance of the Lions, performed with all the ancient ceremonies. Thus Yah Chieng caters to the people's taste for spectacle and tradition. It is the only time when the great gates are opened and the public is admitted into the large courtyard. But how this can avail us I cannot fathom, for we must bring King Conan with us, and he is pale of skin and round of eye. We cannot possibly disguise him effectively, for he stands out among all men. Of course, we could carry him in a box—"

Conan's rough voice broke into the conversation. "None of that, my friend. To lie unmoving in a coffin, indeed! But this Lion Dance gives me an idea. I have heard of it from travelers. Do not the dancers carry great dresses made for two men, with a lion's head? At the end of the feast, I can slip into the castle. Then I shall be on my own. The only snag is the dancing dress. You have none here, and it would take too long to make one."

"Fate is indeed looking our way," replied the old man gravely. "In Shaulun, a day's journey hence, there is a team that goes to the dance every year with their lion dress. We will make it worth their while to let us borrow it. As for the rest, you speak true. You will have many chances to slip away during the latter part of the feast, for Yah Chieng often plies the rabble with wine, and there arises such confusion and shouting that his swordsmen have to chase everybody out with naked swords. Perhaps this time we can turn the riot to our advantage.

"The swordsmen of the usurper would be surprised to meet sober men with forbidden swords in their hands. Aye, I think we could promise Yah Chieng an unusually lively feast!"

"Not yet," said Leng Chi. "How many can we

154

muster? Yah Chieng has his Two Hundred at instant call, besides his regular troops. Some of the latter might come over to us, did they know what was afoot. But—"

"And we have but a few bits of armor," said another headman. "The troops of the usurper will be scaled and plated like the crayfish of Lake Ho."

As the meager forces that the refugees could put in the field were summed up, faces and voices fell again. Then Conan spoke:

"The other day, Lord Kang, you said something about a troop of Western mercenaries captured by Yah Chieng last year. What is this?"

The old man said: "In the Month of the Hog, a company of fifty came marching out of the west. They said they had served the king of—what was the name of the kingdom? Turan, that is it. But, resenting the scornful way this king's generals treated them, they had deserted and struck out eastward to seek their fortunes in Khitai."

Leng Chi took up the tale. "They passed a few leagues north of here, through the village of Shaulun. They found favor with the villagers because they destroyed a band of robbers, and they did not loot or rape. Therefore the villagers warned them against Yah Chieng. But they would not listen, and marched on to Paikang.

"There, we heard, they offered their swords to Yah Chieng. He feigned acceptance but had other plans in mind. He gave them a feast, at the height of which he had their captain's head cut off and the rest cast into his dungeon."

"Why did he do this?" said Conan.

"It seems he wanted them for sacrifices in some great rite of devilish magic."

"What became of them?"

"At last accounts, they still awaited their doom, though that is three months since."

"How did you hear of it?"

"A woman of Paikang, who had been having a love affair with one of the Two Hundred, fled to Shaulun, and thence the tale came to us."

"Lord Kang," said Conan, "tell me about your palace. I shall need to find my way about it."

Kang Hsiu began drawing lines on the earthen floor of the hut. "You know that the usurper may have changed things since I dwelt therein. But this is how they were in my day. Here stands the main gate; here rises the great hall . . ."

Hours later, plans were made down to the last detail. Kang Hsiu rose and swung his goblet high, the amber liquid swirling in the smoky lamplight. He cried in a ringing voice: "To the future and honor of great Paikang, and may the head of the Snake soon be crushed under the boot of the Avenger!"

An answering shout went up, and Conan made a gesture and drank. His brain whirled with the realization that he was at last within reach of his goal.

Dust rose in choking clouds on the road that ran west from Paikang. Hundreds of Khitans in blue and brown shuffled along it towards the city.

The sun gleamed whitely on the massive marble wall of Paikang. The waters of the moat reflected the white walls, the brown hills, and the blue sky, save where the wakes of a flock of swimming ducks disturbed its surface. Over the walls rose the pagodas of Paikang, their multiple roofs gleaming with glazed tiles of green, blue, and purple and glittering with gilded ornaments at the corners. Golden dragons and lions snarled down from the angles of the battlements surmounting the great gate.

The dusty lines of countryfolk streamed into the gate, afoot and on donkeyback. For once Yah Chieng's soldiers stood back, leaning on their bills and tridents and watching the throng without stopping each one for questioning, search, and extortion. Now and then the drab column was lightened by the brilliant costumes of the dancers. The lion dancers of Shaulun made an especially brave show. The gilded lion mask flashed in the sun, turning its bulging eyes and curling tongue this way and that. The man in the forequarters must have been of unusual stature, for the headpiece of the lion costume towered far above the heads of the Khitans.

Inside the city, the countryfolk poured along a winding avenue toward the palace. Conan, peering through the holes below the lion mask, sniffed the pungent smells of a Khitan city and pricked his ears at its sounds. At first it sounded like a meaningless din, though each horn, bell, whistle, and rattle was used by tradesmen of a particular kind to make themselves known.

Following the crowd, he came to another wall with a great gate standing open in it. The folk poured in. The column divided to flow around a jade screen of carven dragons, ten feet high and thrice as long, and joined again on the other side. They were in the courtyard of Yah Chieng's palace, formerly the seat of the Kang clan.

Pushing, shouting masses pressed against the tables where Yah Chieng's servants ladled out rice stew and rice wine. Many of the guests were already in a stimulated condition; the singsong talk of the crowd rose to a roar. Here a juggler tossed balls and hatchets; there a musician plucked a one-stringed lute and sang plaintive songs, though only those within a few feet of him could hear him.

Conan heard Leng Chi's voice in his ear: "Over this way. The dancing will soon begin. Be not so proficient as to win the prize. It would not forward our plans to have the judge demand that you doff your headpiece to receive it . . ."

The long stone corridor was dark. Deathly silence reigned in its murky depths. Conan slunk stealthily forward like a jungle cat, avoiding the slightest sound, carrying his sword unsheathed. He was clad in a Khitan jacket and silken trousers, bought from a merchant in a border village.

As he had planned, so had things befallen. During the rising turmoil in the courtyard, nobody had noticed by the flickering torchlight that one of the lion dresses was now borne by only one carrier. Shadows and nooks had aided Conan's swift entry. Now he was on his way into the heart of the enemy's stronghold.

His senses were sharpened to the utmost. It was not the first time he had entered the abode of a hostile wizard. Memories of the ghastly things he had met on similar occasions thrust themselves upon his consciousness like attacking demons. All his life, the supernatural had been the one thing that could send tendrils of fear probing into his brain. But with iron self-possession, he shrugged off his atavistic fears and continued his catlike stalk.

The corridor branched. One stairway led up, the other down, hardly discernible in the all-pervading darkness. Conan chose the one leading downward. The plan of the castle was well-learned and locked in his brain.

Yo La-gu, one of Yah Chieng's Two Hundred,

lolled on his bench in the dungeon beneath the citadel of Paikang. His temper was ruffled. Why should he of all men sit here, guarding these milksop western prisoners, while outside the feast was in progress and wine and love were to be had for the asking? A stupid idea of the wizard to keep people prisoner for years, preparing to use them up in some magical stunt, when a single raid on the countryside would fetch as many Khitans in a week! Grumbling, he eased himself off the creaking settle to fetch more wine from his secret hoard. His armor rustled and clanked.

He reached the niche in the wall where he had secreted his bottles and stretched his hand towards it —and that was his last conscious act. Ten steely fingers fastened on his windpipe, crushing his throat, until black unconsciousness swamped his brain, and he sank down in a heap.

Conan surveyed his handiwork with a grim smile. It was good to slay foes again! The old barbarian instincts boiled in his blood, and his lips writhed in the snarl of the hunting beast.

His kill had been so swift and silent that none of the sleeping occupants of the cells had stirred. Conan stooped and tore the bunch of keys from the dead jailor's belt. He tried several of them in the lock of the nearest cell.

At the soft metallic sound, a prisoner turned, shook his head, and opened his eyes. The imprecation on his lips was stifled as he beheld the strange figure at the grille. His astonishment grew as the bars swung inward. In a bound, he was on his feet. He checked his rush, for the light from the wall cresset glinted faintly on the blade in the stranger's right hand. A gesture from the giant cautioned him to silence, and another beckoned him to follow.

In the clear light, the eyes of the prisoner widened in surprise. Conan frowned, searching his memory. At last he said: "Lyco of Khorshemish! Is it you?"

"Aye." Their brawny hands met in a firm grip. The prisoner continued: "By the breasts of Ishtar, Conan, I am struck to the core with astonishment! Are you here with an Aquilonian host to deal with the evil sorcerer, or have you flown on the back of an eagle?"

"Neither, Lyco," came the rumbling reply. "I am here to mete out justice to the yellow cur, true, but I counted on finding my army here. I think I have done so. When we fought as mercenaries, yours was always among the readiest blades."

"Most of the prisoners here are true men and fighters," said the other. "We long only to flesh our steel in those Khitan bravos."

"You will have your chance. Here are the keys to the dungeons; take them and free your men. The armory lies down this corridor; equip your followers with blades and strike! Strike to avenge your own suffering and to free the queen of Aquilonia!" He smiled grimly at Lyco's astounded expression. "Now you know why I'm here. You will find Khitan allies among the throng in the courtyard. Go swiftly."

He was gone again like a haunting phantom. Lyco began to waken his comrades, sending some to open the armory while others busied themselves at the locks of other cell doors.

"By Mitra," murmured Lyco, "the barbarian is a mad one! Traveling across the world to rescue a woman!" But admiration glowed in his eyes as he lookd into the dark mouth of the corridor.

10.   The Lair of the Sorcerer

A VAST, high-ceilinged hall opened at the end of the dank stone corridor. Its square flagstones were covered with dust undisturbed by human feet, but its aura of silence brooded menacingly. Its upper part was lost in darkness. Conan stalked warily over the vast floor toward the opening of another corridor, as if he expected any one of the flagstones to drop out from under him.

A noise like a thunderclap rang with booming crashes between the echoing walls, and a shrill wailing cry made Conan's blood run cold. With a swish of mighty wings, an unearthly being swooped from the upper darkness. Like a stooping hawk it plummeted down towards Conan.

The barbarian flung himself aside barely in time to avoid the razor-sharp claws in the monster's paws. Then his sword swept in a glittering arc. The winged horror flopped away, howling. One arm, severed at the elbow, gushed dark, ill-smelling blood. With a horrible scream it again sprang towards the Cimmerian.

Conan stood his ground. He knew that his only chance lay in a sure thrust through the creature's vitals. Even partly dismembered, it had the strength to tear him to pieces. It was, he was sure, the same thing that had borne off Zenobia long months before.

The monster spread its wings to soar as it sprang. At the last moment, Conan ducked the claws of the remaining hand and put all his strength into a ripping thrust. His blade tore into the black body, as the searching talons ripped the shirt from his back.

With a choking gasp, the monster fell. Conan braced his feet to drag his blade free, dripping with the creature's dark juices.

His hair was sweaty and tangled and his back was bloody from the clawing he had received. But a terrible fire burned unquenched in his eyes as he reached the mouth of the other corridor. Behind him, on the floor of the hall, the monster lay in a pool of brown, staring with sightless yellow eyes toward the darkness from which it had come.

The corridor into which Conan stepped was short and straight. In the distance he saw a door of stone. Cryptic signs of Khitan origin covered its surface. This must be the Tunnel of Death that led to Yah Chieng's private chambers. Beyond that door he would find his foe. Conan's eyes glowed ferally in the darkness, and his hand gripped his hilt with vengeful force.

Suddenly the darkness changed to bright illumination. Red licking flames arose from the floor in a hellish wall. Their writhing tongues reached up to the ceiling, and they burst toward Conan in hungry spouts of burning death. He could feel their terrible heat on his face and arms, and his clothes began to smolder. Sweat ran down his face. As he wiped his brow with the back of his hand, a piece of metal rasped his skin.

The ring of Rakhamon again! He had forgotten it in his single-minded determination. Would it prove potent against the strength of the yellow wizard?

He swept his hand through the licking flames. A crash, like the beating of a thousand cymbals, reverberated in the corridor. The flames fell tinkling to the floor, like shards of glass. The rest of the fire was suddenly stiff and cold, like coagulated colors of evil.

Conan hurdled the fossilized fire in a mighty leap and advanced toward the door of stone. He felt irresistible. Vast confidence surged within him, and his hand was raised to smite with the ring of power.

The cold stone altar was chill to Zenobia's warm-blooded body. Her hands twisted futilely in their iron bonds; her feet were chained together and fastened to a ring in the floor. Her splendid body lay stretched out upon the stone. Nearby, her tormentor busied himself at a long, dark table, cluttered with curious implements, phials and boxes and rolls of moldering parchment. His straggly beard showed from under his hood.

The ceiling of the large room was so lofty that Zenobia could not even see it. She almost sobbed with despair, but the steely self-control that had carried her through all these months of captivity held her emotions in check.

She thought of Conan, her spouse, and her heart was near to bursting with longing and sorrow. Yah Chieng had told her, time and again, that Conan had set out single-handed to save her. By what occult arts the wizard had gained this knowledge she did not know. By now her beloved Conan might lie dead upon the Turanian steppe, or he might have been captured and slain by wild Himelian tribesmen. Many powerful men in the eastern lands had no cause to love him.

This noon, the yellow wizard's henchmen had come to her cell and dragged her to this chamber. Here they had chained her to this horrible altar. She had been alone with the Khitan sorcerer since then. He, however, ignored her and pottered about, mumbling incantations from musty volumes, leaving her thoughts to dwell upon the ghastly fate awaiting her.

Now the evil one approached. Light glinted from the oddly-curved blade in his hand. Dark and cryptic symbols were engraved upon it, and his face was taut with evil expectation.

Despairing, she commended her soul to Mitra.

Then the heavy stone door to the room burst inward. With the crash of a hundred falling castles, it fell to the floor in crumpling shards of shattered porphyry. Dust rose like a storm cloud at its fall.

A tall and powerful man stood in the opening, a brawny giant with a square-cut mane of black hair, his blue eyes flashing with kingly wrath. The lights gleamed on the blade in his hand.

Zenobia's heart almost tore itself out of her breast with tearful joy. At last he had come! Her champion! Conan!

With silent and terrible ferocity, the Cimmerian charged at the yellow necromancer. He had taken in the scene at a glance. The sight of Zenobia's body, readied for sacrifice, showed he had not come an instant too soon.

Suddenly, before his eyes, Zenobia rose from the altar, freed from her bonds. And then it was no longer Zenobia, but a huge tiger. Its growl reverberated in the hall as it sprang for Conan with unsheathed claws and slavering jaws. As Conan swung up his tulwar for a decapitating slash, the tiger changed into a moldering skeleton in a dark-green, hooded robe. A bony hand gripped Conan's wrist with a numbing clutch.

With a snarl, Conan tore his tulwar from the entangling folds of the green robe to smash the grinning skull into a thousand fragments. Then he felt a burning sensation upon his middle finger. It felt as if his finger were on fire. The magical ring glowed with an unearthly blue luminescence that sent smarting pains shooting into his brain. He tore the ring sizzling from his flesh and dropped it. Then came a ringing peal of evil laughter from the lips of Yah Chieng.

The Khitan wizard stood with arms stretched over his head. His wizened lips mumbled incessantly, and the lights burned lower in the cressets. Conan shook his head numbly; he had not yet recovered from the shock he had received.

Apathetically, he saw a blue mist rising from the floor around him. It rose with lethal slowness, enveloping him in its dim folds. Although his head seemed to be clearing, he was now wholly enshrouded in fog. He tried to move, but it was like walking in cold honey. He could hardly raise his feet. The breath burst in racking gasps from his lungs, and sweat ran down his face.

The mist darkened still more. Now he began to see visions in the shifting blue wisps. He saw friends of old and fair women, knights on horses and gilded kings. Then these forms changed into enemies of old, and these in turn were transformed into shapes of horror. All the monsters feared by man since he first crawled from the sea whirled in endless succession before his sight, and they came closer and closer. Their strangling hands reached out to crush his throat; their glowing eyes sought to draw the soul from his body to Hell and damnation.

Conan's whole being revolted in horror. His muscles knotted in tremendous efforts, but the power of the mist was greater. The tugging at his mind, at the inner core of his consciousness, became unbearable. He was overwhelmed by the certainty of defeat. Darkness and evil would triumph in the world despite all his efforts. His ensorceled soul would grovel on the floors of Hell in black eternity.

He felt the last strains of consciousness slipping out of his grip.

Then he seemed to see, superimposed on the grinning and slavering waifs of darkness, the picture of a great hall. Giant logs were its walls, and the rafters were as thick as four men, but gloom pervaded it. Dark and somber men in gray mail stood about a throne. Upon the throne sat a black-haired king, tall and moody, with black eyes in an austere and merciless face. And the voice of this king reached out to his mind:

"Man of Cimmeria! You are a son of Crom, and he will not let you suffer eternal damnation! You have always been true to him in your heart, and the black arts of the East shall not have your soul!"

The dark eyes of the god burned. He stretched out his powerful hand, and a great light burst from it. With the light, Conan felt all his old power surge back into his body. The blue mist thinned and curled away. The demons departed in chattering fear and frenzy, and the king of Aquilonia strode forward unhindered.

Fear came into the eyes of Yah Chieng, as he clutched the sacrificial knife and swung it over his head. Zenobia saw it whirling over her. Then a heavy body brought the wizard crashing to the floor in a flurry of limbs and flowing robes.

Conan had hurled himself in a mighty tiger's leap over the altar. The Cimmerian's terrible whisper was cold as ice:

"At last we meet, you yellow dog! Your days of magic are numbered. The gods have doomed you, and your black powers are broken!"

As Conan's death grip tightened, Yah Chieng gibbered in terror.

"Do you hear the shouts and the clash of arms? Do you see the fires? Your swordsmen are being cut down by the prisoners from the dungeons and by the people of Paikang! Your bloody empire is crashing in ruins. To blackest Hell I send you, cur, and may you rot there forever!"

Conan's muscles swelled in an effort of vengeful fury. There was a crack, and the Cimmerian rose panting from the flopping corpse.

His shirt was burnt and torn away, his back was furrowed with scratches, and his eyebrows were singed. But he went up to the altar and exerted his strength in one more gigantic effort. The chains holding the woman tinkled broken to the floor.

As the victorious host came shouting and cheering through the door, they found him embracing his lovely queen with all the ardor of a man in love for the first time.

And that night Conan sacrificed to Crom, god of the black-haired Cimmerian race, for the second time in twenty-five years.

Epilogue

Two RIDERS sat their mounts on the endless, dry-grass steppe. One was a giant, armored in mail hauberk and steel casque, a long, straight sword at his side. The other was a slim, straight woman in the riding garb of a woman of the Eastern nomads, a double-curved Khitan bow in her hand. In front of them, on the ground, lay two inert figures in widening pools of crimson, their spired helmets and gaudy turbans dusty. A small cloud to the east bespoke the mad flight of their riderless horses.

"Outriders of a Turanian troop, Zenobia," muttered the mailed giant. "Ill fortune that they should come across us when our horses are spent and we have many miles to cover ere we reach safety. Too bad, too, that one of them got away."

"Let us not tarry," answered the clear voice of the woman. "We must ride westward as far as we can. Who knows? There may be a chance of escape."

Conan shrugged his broad shoulders and swung his mount about. The short rest had revived the animals, which went into a gallop towards the western horizon, where the mountains were yet hardly discernible despite the clear air and blazing sun.

"You do not know the Hyrkanians," growled Conan. "They're like a pack of hunting dogs. They never let go unless you slay the whole lot."

"But perhaps their main force is far away. We might still win to the woodlands."

"I doubt it. Turanian outriders never lose touch with their column. I learned their tricks when I soldiered with them. They ride in a column over the steppe, and when they get wind of their prey they form into line, charge on well-rested mounts, fling their wings forward, and catch their quarry in a vice. Curse my luck! We've come without mishap so far, and now we're caught almost on our threshold!"

The horses began to falter. Conan wrenched his bridle to keep his mount's head up. Grimly he drew rein, swung his animal about, and shaded his eyes, looking eastward.

A dust-cloud filled the horizon. Glints of metal flashed now and then, and the ground trembled to the thunder of hooves. Conan clenched his teeth and let his sword whistle in the air. His fighting smile was on his lips, and Zenobia looked upon him with love and devotion. If this was to be his last stand, so must it be, and he would make a fight that would put many a hero tale to shame. His blue eyes smoldered with fighting lust, and his fingers gripped the sword hilt with terrible force.

The stormy dust cloud drew nearer with every beat of their hearts. Now they could see the long line of riders, stretching far to the right and left. In the center rode a gaudy figure in gold and scarlet, and beside him a smaller figure in silken robes. At the sight of the latter, Conan stiffened in the saddle and sharpened his eagle's sight. He started, and a curse sounded from between his teeth.

Zenobia had her bow strung and an arrow nocked. She flung a questioning glance at the king.

"That she-devil Thanara!" snarled the king. "Our

169

bat-winged friend saved her from the Zhurazi, and now she rises up to trap me again!"

The riders were now near enough for their long-drawn war cries to be heard. Spear points were lowered in a glittering wave; the ground shook under thundering hooves. Conan flexed his muscles and prepared grimly to meet the attack.

Suddenly, the headlong pace of the attackers slackened. Their horses milled about, and the symmetry of the charging line was broken. Conan swung about in the saddle to see what had caused this sudden check.

The sun flashed blindingly on polished armor, visored salades, couched lances, and whirling swords. In full irresistible charge, four thousand Hyborian knights raced toward the Turanians, the banner of Aquilonia at the tip of their steel-shod wedge.

The Aquilonian ranks parted to sweep around Conan and his queen, then smote the milling ranks of the Turanians with the crushing force of a thunder-stroke. That charge bowled over men and horses by the hundreds, and the knights of Aquilonia raged like tigers among the enemy. Filled with lust of battle, Conan flung himself into the press. His sword crashed down upon the helm of a tall Turanian lancer and rolled him out of the saddle. Like a flash, the king of Aquilonia left his own spent horse and mounted the Turanian's charger. He drove straight for the center of his enemies, and his flashing sword cut a bloody path of death before him.

He smashed in the side of an archer aiming at him at short range, sending the man to the ground like a crumpled doll. Then he faced the amir.

"We meet again, barbarian dog," shouted the tall man in gilt and red. "Your head shall hang from the wall of the lady Thanara's castle!"

170

"I see you got over that last knock on the head," roared the Cimmerian, trading blows with expert ease and controlled ferocity. "You're a fit follower of that treacherous doxy. Rot in Hell!"

His flashing blade redoubled its force and speed. Ardashir's parries failed at last. The heavy steel shore through mail and flesh and bone. The Turanian officer fell to the ground, almost hewn in twain.

Conan paused and looked around. The ground was strewn with dead men in spired helmets and baggy breeches. Although the Aquilonians had suffered a few losses, most of the five thousand Turanians lay still on the steppe. The gleaming lines of the Western knights converged inwards to where there was still some fighting. The remaining Turanians threw down their arms and asked for quarter, all but a few who had fled from the press in time and were now dwindling to specks on the grassy horizon. Conan smiled grimly and looked about for Zenobia.

Only the lightning reflexes of his barbarian muscles saved him. An arrow whizzed past. At the last moment, he caught the menacing gesture of a drawn bow from the corner of his eye and threw himself aside. Thirty feet away, Thanara, her face contorted with rage, fitted another shaft to the string. She drew the bow taut—then, with a *thunk*, an arrow buried itself in her breast, and she fell limply from the saddle. Beside Conan, Zenobia reined in her horse, grimly surveying the result of her marksmanship.

"No man ever had a better wife and no king a better queen!" thundered Conan, lifting her from her horse to put her on his saddle horn.

The fighting was over. Two knights in dusty armor rode up to the king, raised their visors, and bowed.

"Prospero! Trocero!" The dust flew in clouds as

171

Conan's fist slapped their steel-clad shoulders in greeting. "You came in the nick of time, or those dogs would have made it hot for us. How came you hither? I can hardly believe my eyes!"

Prospero, slim and straight and clear-eyed, answered: "Pelias directed us. Since you left, I have visited him often. By occult means he has divined your success and return. He foresaw that you would be attacked here on the border, and we set out to prevent it. Even so, we lost our way in the Corinthian hills, and it was lucky we did not come too late."

"And what of our kingdom, Trocero?"

"Sire, the people hope and long for your return. As we rode out of Tarantia, we were followed by as many blessings as a Poitainian may ever hope to receive. We are at peace, and no one has dared to attack us. The crops are plentiful, and the land was never so prosperous. We lack but the presence of our king and queen to brim the cup of good fortune and happiness."

"Well spoken, my friend! But who comes yonder? Blast me, if it isn't Pelias!"

It was indeed the wizard, tall and lean and gray-haired, with a smile on his lips and his silken robes fluttering.

"Welcome back, King Conan," he said sincerely. "Many moons have passed since we sat in conclave in my tower. You have freed the world of an avid monster, and happier days lie before us."

"I owe you thanks, Pelias, both for this timely aid and for the loan of this bauble." Conan took the ring of Rakhamon from his pouch. "You may have it back. It served me well a couple of times, but I hope I shall never have use for the like of it again."

For the last time he surveyed the gory battleground.

Then he swung his horse about and rode westward at the head of his knights.

In an undertone he muttered to Prospero beside him: "Confound it, my throat is dry as the floor of Hell from all this talking! Have you no wine in your saddle flask?"

THE HYBORIAN AGE.

by
Robert E. Howard

FIVE HUNDRED YEARS LATER [that is, after the reign of Conan the Great—de C.] the Hyborian civilization was swept away. Its fall was unique in that it was not brought about by internal decay, but by the growing power of the barbarian nation and the Hyrkanians. The Hyborian peoples were overthrown while their vigorous culture was in its prime.

Yet it was Aquilonia's greed which brought about that overthrow, though indirectly. Wishing to extend their empire, her kings made war on their neighbors. Zingara, Argos, and Ophir were annexed outright, with the western cities of Shem, which had, with their more eastern kindred, recently thrown off the yoke of Koth. Koth itself, with Corinthia and the eastern Shemitish tribes, was forced to pay Aquilonia tribute and lend aid in wars. An ancient feud had existed between Aquilonia and Hyperborea, and the latter now marched to meet the armies of her western rival. The plains of the Border Kingdom were the scene of a great and savage battle, in which the northern hosts were utterly defeated and retreated into their snowy fastnesses, whither the victorious Aquilonians did not pursue them. Nemedia, which had successfully resisted the western kingdom for centuries, now drew Brythunia and Zamora, and secretly, Koth, into an alliance which bade fair to crush the rising empire. But before their armies could join in battle, a new enemy appeared in the east, as the Hyrkanians made their first real thrust at the western world. Reinforced by adventurers from east of Vilayet, the riders of Turan swept over Zamora, devastated eastern Corinthia, and were met on the plains of Brythunia by the Aquilonians, who defeated them and hurled them flying eastward. But the back of the alliance was broken, and Nemedia took the defensive in future wars, aided occasionally by Brythunia, and Hyperborea, and, secretly as usual, by Koth. This defeat of the Hyrkanians showed the nations the real power of the western kingdom, whose splendid armies were augmented by mercenaries, many of them recruited among the alien Zingarans, and the barbaric Picts and Shemites. Zamora was reconquered from the Hyrkanians, but the people discovered that they had merely exchanged an eastern master for a western master. Aquilonian soldiers were quartered there, not only to protect the ravaged country, but also to keep the people in subjection. The Hyrkanians were not convinced; three more invasions burst upon the Zamorian borders, and the lands of Shem, and were hurled back by the Aquilonians, though the Turanian armies grew larger as hordes of steel-clad riders rode out of the east, skirting the southern extremity of the inland sea.

But it was in the West that a power was growing, destined to throw down the kings of Aquilonia from their high places. In the north there was incessant bickering along the Cimmerian borders between the black-haired warriors and the Nordheimr; and the Æsir, between wars with the Vanir, assailed Hyperborea and pushed back the frontier, destroying city after city. The Cimmerians also fought the Picts and Bossonians impartially and several times raided into Aquilonia itself, but their wars were less invasions than mere plundering forays.

But the Picts were growing amazingly in population and power. By a strange twist of fate, it was largely due to the efforts of one man, and he an alien, that they set their feet upon the ways that led to eventual empire. This man was Arus, a Nemedian priest, a natural-born reformer. What turned his mind toward the Picts is not certain, but this much is history—he determined to go into the western wilderness and modify the rude ways of the heathen by the introduction of the gentle worship of Mitra. He was not daunted by the grisly tales of what had happened to traders and explorers before him, and by some whim of fate he came among the people he sought, alone and unarmed, and was not instantly speared.

The Picts had benefited by contact with Hyborian civilization, but they had always fiercely resisted that contact. That is to say, they had learned to work crudely in copper and tin, which was found scantily in their country, and for which latter metal they raided into the mountains of Zingara, or traded hides, whale's teeth, walrus tusks, and such few things as savages have to trade. They no longer lived in caves and tree shelters, but built tents of hides and crude huts, copied from those of the Bossonians. They still lived mainly by the chase, since their wilds swarmed with game of all sorts, and the rivers and sea with fish, but they had learned how to plant grain, which they did sketchily, preferring to steal it from their neighbors the Bossonians and Zingarans. They dwelt in clans, which were generally at feud with one another, and their simple customs were bloodthirsty and utterly inexplicable to a civilized man, such as Arus of Nemedia. They had no direct contact with the Hyborians, since the Bossonians acted as a buffer between them. But Arus maintained that they were capable of progress, and events proved the truth of his assertion—though scarcely in the way he meant.

Arus was fortunate in being thrown in with a chief of more than usual intelligence—Gorm by name. Gorm cannot be explained, any more than Genghis Khan, Othman, Attila, or any of those individuals, who, born in naked lands among untutored barbarians, yet possess the instinct for conquest and empire-building. In a sort of bastard Bossonian, the priest made the chief understand his purpose, and though extremely puzzled, Gorm gave him permission to remain among his tribe unbutchered—a case unique in the history of the race. Having learned the language, Arus set himself to work to eliminate the more unpleasant phases of Pictish life—such as human sacrifice, blood feud, and the burning alive of captives. He harangued Gorm at length, whom he found to be an interested if unresponsive listener. Imagination reconstructs the scene—the black-haired chief, in his tiger skins and necklace of human teeth, squatting on the dirt floor of the wattle hut, listening intently to the eloquence of the priest, who probably sat on a carven, skin-covered block of mahogany provided in his honor —clad in the silken robes of a Nemedian priest, gesturing with his slender white hands as he expounded the eternal rights and justices which were the truths of Mitra. Doubtless he pointed with repugnance at the rows of skulls which adorned the walls of the hut and urged Gorm to forgive his enemies instead of putting their bleached remnants to such use. Arus was the highest product of an innately artistic race, refined by centuries of civilization; Gorm had behind him a heritage of a hundred thousand years of screaming savagery—the pad of the tiger was in his stealthy step, the grip of the gorilla in his black-nailed hands, the fire that burns in a leopard's eyes burned in his.

Arus was a practical man. He appealed to the savage's sense of material gain; he pointed out the power and splendor of the Hyborian kingdoms as an example of the power of Mitra, whose teachings and works had lifted them up to their high places. And he spoke of cities and fertile plains, marble walls and iron chariots, jeweled towers and horsemen in their glittering armor riding to battle. And Gorm, with the unerring instinct of the barbarian, passed over his words regarding gods and their teachings and fixed on the material powers thus vividly described. There in that mud-floored wattle hut, with the silk-robed priest on the mahogany block and the dark-skinned chief crouching in his tiger hides, was laid the foundations of empire.

As has been said, Arus was a practical man. He dwelt among the Picts and found much that an intelligent man could do to aid humanity, even when that humanity was cloaked in tiger skins and wore necklaces of human teeth. Like all priests of Mitra, he was instructed in many things. He found that there were vast deposits of iron ore in the Pictish hills, and he taught the natives to mine, smelt, and work it into implements—agricultural implements, as he fondly believed. He instituted other reforms, but these were the most important things he did: he instilled in Gorm a desire to see the civilized lands of the world; he taught the Picts how to work in iron; and he established contact between them and the civilized world. At the chief's request, he conducted him and some of his warriors through the Bossonian marches, where the honest villagers stared in amazement, into the glittering outer world.

Arus no doubt thought that he was making converts right and left, because the Picts listened to him and refrained from smiting him with their copper axes. But the Pict was little calculated seriously to regard teachings which bade him forgive his enemy and abandon the warpath for the ways of honest drudgery. It has been said that he lacked artistic sense; his whole nature led to war and slaughter. When the priest talked of the glories of the civilized nations, his dark-skinned listeners were intent, not on the ideals of his religion, but on the loot which he unconsciously described in the narration of rich cities and shining lands. When he told how Mitra aided certain kings to overcome their enemies, they paid scant heed to the miracles of Mitra, but they hung on the description of battle lines, mounted knights, and maneuvers of archers and spearmen. They harkened with keen dark eyes and inscrutable countenances, and they went their ways without comment, and heeding with flattering intentness his instructions as to the working of iron and kindred arts.

Before his coming, they had filched steel weapons and armor from the Bossonians and Zingarans or had hammered out their own crude arms from copper and bronze. Now a new world opened to them, and the clang of sledges reëchoed throughout the land. And Gorm, by virtue of this new craft, began to assert his dominance over other clans, partly by war, partly by craft and diplomacy, in which latter art he excelled all other barbarians.

Picts now came and went freely into Aquilonia, under safe-conduct, and they returned with more information as to armor-forging and sword-making.

More, they entered Aquilonia's mercenary armies, to the unspeakable disgust of the sturdy Bossonians. Aquilonia's kings toyed with the idea of playing the Picts against the Cimmerians and possibly thus destroying both menaces, but they were too busy with their policies of aggression in the south and east to pay much heed to the vaguely-known lands of the West, from which more and more stocky warriors swarmed to take service among the mercenaries.

These warriors, their service completed, went back to their wilderness with good ideas of civilized warfare and that contempt for civilization which arises from familiarity with it. Drums began to beat in the hills, gathering-fires smoked on the heights, and savage sword makers hammered their steel on a thousand anvils. By intrigues and forays too numerous and devious to enumerate, Gorm became chief of chiefs and the nearest approach to a king the Picts had had in thousands of years. He had waited long; he was past middle age. But now he moved against the frontiers, not in trade, but in war.

Arus saw his mistake too late; he had not touched the soul of the pagan, in which lurked the hard fierceness of all the ages. His persuasive eloquence had not caused a ripple in the Pictish conscience. Gorm wore a corselet of silvered mail now instead of the tiger skin, but underneath he was unchanged—the everlasting barbarian, unmoved by theology or philosophy, his instincts fixed unerringly on rapine and plunder.

The Picts burst on the Bossonian frontiers with fire and sword, not clad in tiger skins and brandishing copper axes as of yore, but in scale mail, wielding weapons of keen steel. As for Arus, he was brained by a drunken Pict while making a last effort to undo the work he had unwittingly done. Gorm was not without gratitude; he caused the skull of the slayer to be set on the top of the priest's cairn. And it is one of the grim ironies of the universe that the stones which covered Arus' body should have been adorned with that last touch of barbarity—above a man to whom violence and blood vengeance were revolting.

But the newer waepons and mail were not enough to break the lines. For years the superior armaments and sturdy courage of the Bossonians held the invaders at bay, aided, when necessary, by imperial Aquilonian troops. During this time, the Hyrkanians came and went and Zamora was added to the empire.

Then treachery from an unexpected source broke the Bossonian lines. Before chronicling this treachery, it might be well to glance briefly at the Aquilonian Empire. Always a rich kingdom, untold wealth had been rolled in by conquest, and the sumptuous splendor had taken the place of simple and hardy living. But degeneracy had not yet sapped the kings and the people; though clad in silks and cloth-of-gold, they were still a vital, virile race. But arrogance was supplanting their former simplicity. They treated less powerful people with growing contempt, levying more and more tributes on the conquered. Argos, Zingara, Ophir, Zamora, and the Shemite countries were treated as subjugated provinces, which was especially galling to the proud Zingarans, who often revolted despite savage retaliations.

Koth was practically tributary, being under Aquilonia's "protection" against the Hyrkanians. But Nemedia the western empire had never been able to subdue, although the latter's triumphs were of the defensive sort and were generally attained with the aid of Hyperborean armies. During this period Aquilonia's only defeats were: her failure to annex

Nemedia; the rout of an army by the Æsir. Just as the Hyrkanians found themselves unable to withstand the heavy cavalry charges of the Aquilonians, so the latter, invading the snow countries, were overwhelmed by the ferocious hand-to-hand fighting of the Nordics. But Aquilonia's conquests were pushed to the [Styx or] Nilus, where a Stygian army was defeated with great slaughter, and the king of Stygia sent tribute —once at least—to divert invasion of his kingdom. Brythunia was reduced in a series of whirlwind wars, and preparations were made to subjugate the ancient rival at last—Nemedia.

With their glittering hosts greatly increased by mercenaries, the Aquilonians moved against their old-time foe, and it seemed as if the thrust were destined to crush the last shadow of Nemedian independence. But contentions arose between the Aquilonians and their Bossonian auxiliaries.

As the inevitable result of imperial expansion, the Aquilonians had become haughty and intolerant. They derided the ruder, unsophisticated Bossonians, and hard feeling grew between them—the Aquilonians despising the Bossonians, and the latter resenting the attitude of their masters—who now boldly called themselves such and treated the Bossonians like conquered subjects, taxing them exorbitantly and conscripting them for their wars of territorial expansion —wars the profits of which the Bossonians shared little. Scarcely enough men were left in the marches to guard the frontier, and hearing of Pictish outrages in their homelands, whole Bossonian regiments quit the Nemedian campaign and marched to the western frontier, where they defeated the dark-skinned invaders in a great battle.

This desertion, however, was the direct cause of the Aquilonia's defeat by the desperate Nemedians, and brought down on the Bossonians the cruel wrath of the imperialists—intolerant and short-sighted as imperialists invariably are. Aquilonian regiments were secretly brought to the borders of the marches, the Bossonian chiefs were invited to attend a great conclave, and, in the guise of an expedition against the Picts, bands of savage Shemitish soldiers were quartered among the unsuspecting villagers. The unarmed chiefs were massacred, the Shemites turned on their stunned hosts with torch and sword, and the armored imperial hosts were hurled ruthlessly on the unsuspecting people. From north to south the marches were ravaged, and the Aquilonian armies marched back from the borders, leaving a ruined and devastated land behind them.

And then the Pictish invasion burst in full power along those borders. It was no mere raid but the concerted rush of a whole nation, led by chiefs who had served in Aquilonian armies and planned and directed by Gorm—an old man now but with the fire of his fierce ambition undimmed. This time there were no strong walled villages in their path, manned by sturdy archers, to hold back the rush until the imperial troops could be brought up. The remnants of the Bossonians were swept out of existence, and the blood-mad barbarians swarmed into Aquilonia, looting and burning, before the legions, warring again with the Nemedians, could be marched into the west. Zingara seized this opportunity to throw off the yoke, which example was followed by Corinthia and the Shemites. Whole regiments of mercenaries and vassals mutinied and marched back to their own countries, looting and burning as they went. The Picts surged irresistibly eastward, and host after host was trampled beneath their feet. Without their Bossonian archers, the Aquilonians found themselves unable to cope with the terrible arrow storm of the barbarians. From all parts of the empire, legions were recalled to resist the onrush, while from the wilderness horde after horde swarmed forth, in apparently inexhaustible supply. And in the midst of this chaos, the Cimmerians swept down from their hills, completing the ruin. They looted cities, devastated the country, and retired into the hills with their plunder, but the Picts occupied the land they had overrun. And the Aquilonian Empire went down in fire and blood.

Then again the Hyrkanians rode from the blue East. The withdrawal of the imperial legions from Zamora was their incitement. Zamora fell easy prey to their thrusts, and the Hyrkanian king established his captial in the largest city of the country. This invasion was from the ancient Hyrkanian kingdom of Turan, on the shores of the inland sea, but another, more savage Hyrkanian thrust came from the north. Hosts of steel-clad riders galloped around the northern extremity of the inland sea, traversed the icy deserts, entered the steppes, driving the aborigines before them and launched themselves against the western kingdoms. These newcomers were not at first allies with the Turanians but skirmished with them as with the Hyborians; now drifts of eastern warriors bickered and fought until all were united under a great chief, who came riding from the very shores of the eastern ocean. With no Aquilonian armies to oppose them, they were invincible. They swept over and subjugated Brythunia and devastated southern Hyperborea and Corinthia. They swept into the Cimmerian hills, driving the black-haired barbarians before them; but among the hills, where cavalry was less effectual, the Cimmerians turned on them, and only a disorderly retreat, at the end of a whole day of bloody fighting, saved the Hyrkanian hosts from complete annihilation.

While these events had been transpiring, the kingdoms of Shem had conquered their ancient master, Koth, and had been defeated in an attempted invasion of Stygia. But scarcely had they completed their degradation of Koth, when they were overrun by the Hyrkanians and found themselves subjugated by sterner masters than the Hyborians had ever been. Meanwhile the Picts had made themselves complete masters of Aquilonia, practically blotting out the inhabitants. They had broken over the borders of Zingara, and thousands of Zingarans, fleeing the slaughter into Argos, threw themselves on the mercy of the westward-sweeping Hyrkanians, who settled them in Zamora as subjects. Behind them as they fled, Argos was enveloped in the flame and slaughter of Pictish conquest, and the slayers swept into Ophir and clashed with the westward-riding Hyrkanians. The latter, after their conquest of Shem, had overthrown a Stygian army at the Nilus and overrun the country as far south as the black kingdom of Amazon, of whose people they brought back thousands as captives, settling them among the Shemites. Possibly they would have completed their conquests in Stygia, adding it to their widening empire, but for the fierce thrusts of the Picts against their western conquests.

Nemedia, unconquerable by Hyborians, reeled between the riders of the East and the swordsmen of the West, when a tribe of Æsir, wandering down from their snowy lands, came into the kingdom and were engaged as mercenaries; they proved such able warriors that they not only beat off the Hyrkanians but halted the eastward advance of the Picts.

185

The world at that time presents some such picture: a vast Pictish empire, wild, rude, and barbaric, stretches from the coasts of Vanaheim in the north to the southernmost shores of Zingara. It stretches east to include all Aquilonia except Gunderland, the northernmost province, which, as a separate kingdom in the hills, survived the fall of the empire and still maintained its independence. The Pictish empire also includes Argos, Ophir, the western part of Koth, and the westernmost lands of Shem. Opposed to this barbaric empire is the empire of the Hyrkanians, of which the northern boundaries are the ravaged lines of Hyperborea, and the southern, the deserts south of the lands of Shem. Zamora, Brythunia, the Border Kingdom, Corinthia, most of Koth, and all the eastern lands of Shem are included in this empire. The borders of Cimmeria are intact; neither Pict nor Hyrkanian has been able to subdue those warlike barbarians. Nemedia, dominated by the Æsir mercenaries, resists all invasions. In the north Nordheim, Cimmeria, and Nemedia separate the conquering races, but in the south, Koth has become a battleground where Picts and Hyrkanians war incessantly. Sometimes the eastern warriors expel the barbarians from the kingdom entirely; again the plains and cities are in the hands of the western invaders. In the far south Stygia, shaken by the Hyrkanian invasion, is being encroached upon by the great black kingdoms. And in the far north, the Nordic tribes are restless, warring continually with the Cimmerians and sweeping the Hyperborean frontiers.

Gorm was slain by Hialmar, a chief of the Nemedian Æsir. He was a very old man, nearly a hundred years old. In the seventy-five years which had elapsed since he first heard the tale of empires from the lips of Arus—a long time in the life of a man, but a brief space in the tale of nations—he had welded an empire from straying savage clans, he had overthrown a civilization. He who had been born in a mud-walled, wattle-roofed hut, in his old age sat on golden thrones and gnawed joints of beef presented to him on golden dishes by naked slave girls who were the daughters of kings. Conquest and the acquiring of wealth altered not the Pict; out of the ruins of the crushed civilization no new culture arose phoenixlike. The dark hands which shattered the artistic glories of the conquered never tried to copy them. Though he sat among the glittering ruins of shattered palaces and clad his hard body in the silks of vanquished kings, the Pict remained the eternal barbarian, ferocious, elemental, interested only in the naked primal principles of life, unchanging, unerring in his instincts which were all for war and plunder, and in which arts and the cultured progress of humanity had no place. Not so with the Æsir who settled in Nemedia. These soon adopted many of the ways of their civilized allies, modified powerfully, however, by their own intensely virile and alien culture.

For a short age, Pict and Hyrkanian snarled at each other over the ruins of the world they had conquered. Then began the glacier ages and great Nordic drift. Before the southward-moving ice fields the northern tribes drifted, driving kindred clans before them. The Æsir blotted out the ancient kingdom of Hyperborea and across its ruins came to grips with the Hyrkanians. Nemedia had already become a Nordic kingdom, ruled by the descendants of the Æsir mercenaries. Driven before the onrushing tides of Nordic invasion, the Cimmerians were on the march, and neither army nor city stood before them. They surged across and completely destroyed the kingdom of Gunderland, and marched across ancient Aquilonia, hewing their irresistible way through the Pictish hosts. They defeated the Nordic-Nemedians and sacked some of their cities but did not halt. They continued eastward, overthrowing an Hyrkanian army on the borders of Brythunia.

Behind them, hordes of Æsir and Vanir swarmed into the lands, and the Pictish empire reeled beneath their strokes. Nemedia was overthrown, and the half-civilized Nordics fled before their wilder kinsmen, leaving the cities of Nemedia ruined and deserted. These fleeing Nordics, who had adopted the name of the older kingdom and to whom the term Nemedian henceforth refers, came into the ancient land of Koth, expelled both Picts and Hyrkanians, and aided the people of Shem to throw off the Hyrkanian yoke. All over the western world, the Picts and Hyrkanians were staggering before this younger, fiercer people. A band of Æsir drove the eastern riders from Brythunia and settled there themselves, adopting the name for themselves. The Nordics who had conquered Hyperborea assailed their eastern enemies so savagely that the dark-skinned descendants of the Lemurians retreated into the steppes, pushed irresistibly back toward Vilayet.

Meanwhile the Cimmerians, wandering southeastward, destroyed the ancient Hyrkanian kingdom of Turan and settled on the southwestern shores of the inland sea. The power of the eastern conquerors was broken. Before the attacks of the Nordheimr and the Cimmerians, they destroyed all their cities, butchered such captives as were not fit to make the long march, and then, herding thousands of slaves before them, rode back into the mysterious East, skirting the northern edge of the sea, and vanishing from western history until they rode out of the east again, thousands

188

of years later, as Huns, Mongols, Tartars, and Turks. With them in their retreat went thousands of Zamorians and Zingarans, who were settled together far to the east, formed a mixed race, and emerged ages afterward as gypsies.

Meanwhile, also, a tribe of Vanir adventurers had passed along the Pictish coast southward, ravaged ancient Zingara, and come into Stygia, which, oppressed by a cruel aristocratic ruling class, was staggering under the thrusts of the black kingdoms to the south. The red-haired Vanir led the slaves in a general revolt, overthrew the reigning class, and set themselves up as a caste of conquerors. They subjugated the northernmost black kingdoms and built a vast southern empire, which they called Egypt. From these red-haired conquerors the earlier Pharaohs boasted descent.

The western world was now dominated by Nordic barbarians. The Picts still held Aquilonia and part of Zingara, and the western coast of the continent. But east to Vilayet, and from the Arctic Circle to the lands of Shem, the only inhabitants were roving tribes of Nordheimr, excepting the Cimmerians, settled in the old Turanian kingdom. There were no cities anywhere, except in Stygia and the lands of Shem; the invading tides of Picts, Hyrkanians, Cimmerians, and Nordics had levelled them in ruins, and the once dominant Hyborians had vanished from the earth, leaving scarcely a trace of their blood in the veins of their conquerors. Only a few names of lands, tribes, and cities remained in the language of the barbarians, to come down through the centuries connected with distorted legend and fable, until the whole history of the Hyborian Age was lost sight of in a cloud of myths and fantasies. Thus in the speech of the gypsies lingered the terms Zingara and Zamora; the Æsir who dominated Nemedia were called Nemedians, and later figured in Irish history; and the Nordics who settled in Brythunia were known as Brythunians, Brythons, or Britons.

There was no such thing, at that time, as a consolidated Nordic empire. As always, the tribes had each its own chief or king, and they fought savagely among themselves. What their destiny might have been will not be known, because another terrific convulsion of the earth, carving out the lands as they are known to moderns, hurled all into chaos again. Great strips of the western coast sank; Vanaheim and western Asgard—uninhabited and glacier-haunted wastes for a hundred years—vanished beneath the waves. The ocean flowed around the mountains of western Cimmeria to form the North Sea; these mountains became the islands later known as England, Scotland, and Ireland, and the waves rolled over what had been the Pictish wilderness and the Bossonian marches. In the North, the Baltic Sea was formed, cutting Asgard into the peninsulas later known as Norway, Sweden, and Denmark, and far to the south the Stygian continent was broken away from the rest of the world, on the line of cleavage formed by the river Nilus in its western trend. Over Argos, western Koth, and the western lands of Shem washed the blue ocean men later called the Mediterranean. But where land sank elsewhere, a vast expanse west of Stygia rose out of the waves, forming the whole western half of the continent of Africa.

The buckling of the land thrust up great mountain ranges in the central part of the northern continent. Whole Nordic tribes were blotted out, and the rest retreated eastward. The territory about the slowly drying inland sea was not affected, and there, on the western shores, the Nordic tribes began a pastoral existence, living in more or less peace with the Cimmerians, and gradually mixing with them. In the west the remnants of the Picts, reduced by the cataclysm once more to the status of stone age savages, began, with the incredible virility of their race, once more to possess the land, until, at a later age, they were overthrown by the westward drift of the Cimmerians and Nordics. This was so long after the breaking-up of the continent that only meaningless legends told of former empires.

This drift comes within the reach of modern history and need not be repeated. It resulted from a growing population which thronged the steppes west of the inland sea—which still later, much reduced in size, was known as the Caspian—to such an extent that migration became an economic necessity. The tribes moved southward, northward, and westward, into those lands now know as India, Asia Minor, and central and western Europe.

They came into these countries as Aryans. But there were variations among these primitive Aryans, some of which are still recognized today, others which have long been forgotten. The blond Achaians, Gauls, and Britons, for instance, were descendants or pure-blooded Æsir. The Nemedians of Irish legendry were the Nemedian Æsir. The Danes were descendants of the pure-blooded Vanir; the Goths—ancestors of the other Scandinavian and Germanic tribes, including the Anglo-Saxons—were descendants of a mixed race whose elements contained Vanir, Æsir, and Cimmerian strains. The Gaels, ancestors of the Irish and Highland Scotch, descended from pure-blooded Cimmerian clans. The Cymric tribes of Britain were a mixed Nordic-Cimmerian race which preceded the purely Nordic Britons into the isles, and thus gave rise to a legend of Gaelic priority. The Cimbri who fought Rome were of the same blood, as well as the Gimmerai of the Assyrians and Grecians, and Gomer of the Hebrews. Other clans of the Cimmerians adventured east of the drying inland sea, and a few centuries later, mixed with Hyrkanian blood, returned westward as Scythians. The original ancestors of the Gaels gave their name to modern Crimea.

The ancient Sumerians had no connection with the western race. They were a mixed people, of Hyrkanian and Shemitish bloods, who were not taken with the conquerors in their retreat. Many tribes of Shem escaped that captivity, and from pure-blooded Shemites, or Shemites mixed with Hyborian or Nordic blood, were descended the Arabs, Israelites, and other straighter-featured Semites. The Canaanites or Alpine Semites traced their descent from Shemitish ancestors mixed with the Kushites settled among them by their Hyrkanian masters; the Elamites were a typical race of this type. The short, thick-limbed Etruscans, base of the Roman race, were descendants of a people of mixed Stygian, Hyrkanian, and Pictish strains and originally lived in the ancient kingdom of Koth. The Hyrkanians, retreating to the eastern shores of the continent, evolved into the tribes later known as Tartars, Huns, Mongols, and Turks.

The origins of other races of the modern world may be similarly traced; in almost every case, older by far than they realize, their history stretches back into the mists of the forgotten Hyborian Age. . . .

CASCA
THE ETERNAL MERCENARY
by Barry Sadler